Amber's

Challenge

BOOK 4

Amber's Challenge

By Helen Haraldsen

Amber's Challenge

Editing, cover design, and formatting by Let's Get Booked:

www.letsgetbooked.com

Paperback ISBN: 978-1-913953-03-4

eBook ISBN: 978-1-913953-04-1

*This book is dedicated to The Pony Club for all they
do to encourage and educate young riders.*

Contents

Secret 1

Dark Horse... 6

Pony Problems 13

Equations 23

Quiet as a Mouse.. 30

Bad Dreams... 37

Sink or Swim 47

Roar 62

All Over 74

There's no I in Team... 81

Unfriended 90

Hunting for Treasure... 99

Horse Whisperer 111

Eye Eye.. 123

Keeping the Faith... 129

All for One and One for All 136

The Calm Before the Storm 147

The Heat is On 158

Rock the Boat.. 167

The Last Laugh 178

An Unexpected Gift 191

Author's Note 202

Acknowledgements.. 205

– One –

Secret

Amber's feet pounded the tarmac. She had found her rhythm, her breathing was deep and regular, and she was ready to make her move. She lengthened her stride and pushed on towards the form of her friend Emily, who wasn't far ahead. Emily's energy was spent and she was flagging. Without looking at her, Amber moved steadily past her, her eyes focused on the remaining runners ahead of her.

With only a couple of weeks left before the Brantfort Pony Club Tetrathlon, Amber was pushing herself to her limit in the running and swimming training. She hadn't told her teammates, or even her parents that she wouldn't be riding Molly in the cross-country phase, and would be taking Honey instead. Although the Fell

1

pony was as reliable as rain in Cumbria, she was guaranteed to pick up a bundle of time faults which could be costly for the team's score. Amber knew that her decision would not prove to be popular.

Just weeks ago, her competition pony Molly had put in an impressive performance around her first ever cross-country course. There had been the small blip where Molly had tried to long-jump the water fence, which resulted in Amber taking a dive into its slimy contents, but everyone agreed this was just a silly mistake due to lack of experience. Overall, Molly had delivered a classy performance, eating up the ground with ease, and now everyone was fully expecting Amber to ride Molly in the team Tetrathlon event.

But there was a problem. Despite slowly developing her confidence in the pony, Amber still didn't trust her. Since JoJo had told her about the gate and slip rail that were part of the Tetrathlon riding test, Amber had known that there was no way she could ride Molly. The last time she had tried to negotiate a gate while mounted on her, Molly had been totally uncooperative. Amber was forced to dismount to open the gate and, when she'd gone to remount, Molly had turned and bolted for home, leaving Amber abandoned and injured on the cold, hard track.

Now, whenever Amber pictured herself trying to do the gate on the cross-country course on an excited pony, or worse, trying to remount after the slip rail, savage claws tightened around her heart and gripped her so tightly she couldn't breathe.

Hating herself for her fear, she plunged on towards the other girls still ahead of her on the cycle track. Mr Pryde, their trainer, was at the front with the strongest two runners: Chelsea from the junior team and Elise from the seniors, egging them on to battle for first place. Amber pushed herself on, overtaking Maia and Isobel. Her breath was rasping now and she could taste blood, but, accepting the punishment, she drove through the pain and accelerated. By the time she reached the end of their marked distance, just behind Chelsea and Elise, for the first time, her legs shook and gave way, tipping her straight on to the path. She lay sprawling and gasping for air, her carnival heartbeat thumping against the path beneath her.

She felt a hand on her back.

"Jeez, Amber, are you alright?" Of course it was Mr Pryde. He was the only one not out of breath. "You put in a terrific effort there; great to see, but try not to injure yourself right before the competition by face planting the tarmac."

Mr Pryde chuckled at his own joke and helped Amber to sit up, but she did not smile or even acknowledge him. He probably thought she was just desperate to win, like he would be. He had no idea of the real reason she was pushing herself so hard.

The need to prove herself was growing and spreading with the urgency of a forest fire, burning a path through her. She *couldn't* disappoint. She was sick of disappointing herself and her parents. Sure, they told her they were proud of her. Proud of her determination and resilience. *What they mean,* she thought, *is that you're not very good at anything but we admire you for trying.* This time she didn't want to be admired for trying. She didn't want pity. Amber wanted to hold her head up and feel equal to her teammates. If she couldn't be the best, at least she could be good enough.

As she sat gasping on the hard tarmac, images of herself grounded by Molly crept into her mind. *Stop it.*

She shook her head, unsure whether she'd spoken out loud. *Not this time.* She forced the memories out and replaced them with her favourite conjuring of the moment. In it, her parents were clapping furiously, her father's eyes brimming with tears of pride as she was handed a huge trophy. Her teammates flanked her, and together they lifted the trophy skywards, blinking as the sun reflected off the silver. Champions.

It was a dream. *But not all dreams are impossible,* Amber constantly reminded herself. For her, it was a beacon. A goal. Not a dream, but something real. *It could happen. It could. It really could.*

– Two –

Dark Horse

The next morning when Amber woke, the aches and pains from the previous day shot through her the moment she tried to turn over to check her alarm clock. As she stiffly reached towards her bedside table, she felt something beside her in bed. Smiling, she abandoned the clock and reached down under the covers where her hand connected with the sleek, warm body of Stig the cat who was curled up beside her. He wasn't allowed upstairs since he'd been locked in a bedroom by accident once and pulled the carpet up in a bid to tunnel under the door. But if he could sneak up without anyone seeing, he loved to cuddle next to Amber. She always wondered how he could breathe under the covers.

The instant she stroked his back, a loud drone of purring set off. It was comforting, and Amber lay there for minutes, not thinking of anything, just enjoying the company of her contented cat. She was grateful for a rest from thinking. It was all she was doing at the moment, her thoughts leapfrogging over each other, pushing and jostling like children in a playground. She'd gone to sleep late last night, only stopping scrolling through the internet on her phone when the battery died. She closed her eyes, drifting back to sleep with a beautifully empty mind.

BEEP BEEP BEEP BEEP BEEP BEEP BEEP BE…

Amber slammed her hand down on the alarm clock. Squinting at the large but blurry green numbers on the screen, she saw it was time to get up. 8am. That reminded her it was Sunday. Good that it wasn't a school day but bad that she'd have to see Molly and endure the heavy weight of guilt that settled on her every time she saw her pony. Would today be the day she told her parents how she felt about Molly? She'd tried several times but couldn't do it. They seemed to think everything was fine now and that Amber was over her early troubles. Given the stress and worry Molly had caused them too, she didn't want to disappoint them, so kept the words locked inside.

Amber flung off her duvet and inched slowly and painfully out of the right side of the bed, not wanting to disturb the sleeping cat on her left. Pulling on a pair of grass green jodhpurs and a long-sleeved grey base layer, Amber shuffled downstairs ready to start the day.

They arrived at Shaw Farm later that morning after Amber had extricated a reluctant Stig from her bed, prising each of his claws out of the bedsheets as he clung on, determined to have a duvet day.

Honey would sometimes refuse to be caught by Mr Anderson, so he started mucking out Molly's stable while Amber and her mum went to bring the Fell ponies in from the field so they could all go on a ride together. It was while she was fastening Pearl's head collar and preparing to lead her towards the field gate that she heard a rattling on the farm track. Looking up over Pearl's neck, she saw Jerry and Caroline Blakely in the silver cattle lorry they used as a horsebox heading towards the farmyard. Amber frowned. She'd seen Oriel, Caroline's horse, in the paddock behind the house as she walked to the Fellies' field... so what was in the lorry?

The ramp was just being lowered as she and her mum led Pearl and Honey into the yard. Curiosity halted Amber and she peered into the gloomy interior of the lorry waiting to see what was within.

A horse the colour of darkness stepped forward. Caroline held it at the top of the ramp, letting it take in its new surroundings before asking it to step down. If it had seen the Fell ponies standing in the yard, it didn't acknowledge them. Even when Molly noticed the newcomer and whinnied loudly, pressing herself eagerly against the stable door, the dark horse merely fluttered its nostrils slightly and allowed itself to be led towards Oriel's stable, next to Molly's.

As the horse walked away, Amber noted that she was a mare. A lean, fit, cocoa coloured thoroughbred. Soon she was in the stable looking over the door, her kind eyes surveying them as they stared back at her. She didn't have a white hair anywhere on her. The only break in her dark chocolate coat was a dun Exmoor pony-esque muzzle. She was plain and had slightly too-large ears for her dainty face, but her stillness intrigued Amber. When

Caroline stepped out of the stable and removed the mare's head collar, Amber couldn't wait to ask her about the new horse.

"Who's this, Caroline? Amber ran through some possible names that might suit this serene mare... Nyx, she thought, the goddess of night, or perhaps Jet as she was sleek and streamlined like a jet. Or maybe Raven or Coco or...

"This is Lady," Caroline said.

"Oh." Amber found the name a little plain and underwhelming compared to the names she'd been imagining. She waited to hear more.

"She's one of my grandad's. He's a racehorse trainer and she's an ex-racer. She's here as she's had a bit of a bad time recently."

"Oh no. Why? What's happened?" Mrs Anderson asked, also clearly interested in the yard's new addition.

"Someone bought her from my grandad, straight off the track. She hadn't had any retraining but the woman said she was experienced and knew what she was doing so he took her word for it. Not long after she got Lady, she took her for a beach ride, and while galloping on the sand, must've run into a soft section. Lady fell and came down on top of her."

Caroline paused to stroke Lady's face, who was still looking quietly over the stable door. "I don't know whether she panicked or if she struggled in the soft sand to get back on her feet, but somehow she managed to kick the woman in the face. Broke her jaw. Lady was sent back to my grandad."

Amber and her mother looked at each other in horror. Mr Anderson had now left Molly's stable to join them in hearing Lady's tale and he gave a low whistle.

"So the word's spread," Caroline continued. "She's been labelled a dangerous horse and now no-one will touch her with a barge pole. My grandad hasn't got room for her so he's given her to me. She's been a good steeplechaser and placed quite a lot, but it's time for her to retire from racing now. He says she hasn't got a bad bone in her body and it was just a terrible accident. I hate to see a good horse written off undeservedly, so I thought, since Oriel's been not-quite-sound recently, I'd give her a rest and concentrate on Lady for this summer."

"Well, we wish you good luck with her," Mrs Anderson said as she led Honey away towards her and Pearl's large shared stable around the corner.

As Amber followed her mother with Pearl, she thought about what Caroline had just told them. *How ironic*, she thought, *that a horse that had broken someone's jaw should be named Lady. Was she a Lady? Or was she another Molly? She might be talented and nice to look at, like Molly, but did that calm exterior mask an unpredictable and explosive nature?* She prayed that Caroline wouldn't get hurt finding out.

But at the same time as feeling concerned for Caroline, her admiration for the young woman rose even further as she recalled Caroline's words. *'I hate to see a good horse written off undeservedly,'* she'd said.

Is that what I'm doing with Molly? Amber wondered. *Writing her off when maybe she just needs another chance? Look at how much she improved when she got her new saddle, because the old one didn't fit her properly. Maybe I shouldn't give up on her just yet. Maybe there's still a chance for us.*

- Three -

🐴

Pony Problems

Mrs Anderson had assumed that Amber would be riding Pearl, since she had caught and groomed her, and that she'd be riding Molly, but Amber took Molly's tack to her stable to get her ready, leaving her parents to prepare the Fell ponies. Mrs Anderson was pleased. Since the Tetrathlon, Amber had been acting strangely with Molly, not engaging with her and turning her attention more towards the Fellies. Mrs Anderson was confused by her behaviour as she'd believed her daughter was gaining in confidence with her new pony, especially after her recent excellent performance at the One Day Event. She knew that she may have been shaken by her fall in the water jump, but she'd been unhurt and had completed the competition in spectacular style. So she couldn't account for her daughter's coolness towards Molly since.

***

As Amber saddled Molly and fastened her girth, ignoring the pony's gnashing teeth – something she always did when her girth was tightened – she ran through the plan in her head. When they got to the forestry gate, if it was closed, she was going to volunteer to get off and open it. Once they were all through, she'd prop it open with the rock so they wouldn't need to deal with it on the way back, and ask her parents to block the gateway with the Fell ponies while she remounted Molly. She was sure that with the company of other ponies, Molly would have no desire to gallop off like she had last time.

Amber needed to get over her phobia of mounting Molly, not for the Tetrathlon, but for her relationship with the pony. If she couldn't trust her, if a sliver of fear lingered, it would be a poison that would become an incurable infection. She needed to do her very best to build a bond with Molly, otherwise there could be no future for them. It was disappointing that the bond hadn't been instant and effortless, like it had been with Pearl and then with Honey, but her internet searches last night had suggested that lots of people experienced what she was going through. It was heartening to know that it was quite common, apparently, for people to experience problems with a new pony, and that these weren't always insurmountable.

She'd read a story about a young girl who got a second pony, as her first wasn't a very good jumper, however the pony was naughty when she got him and threw her off by bucking and broncing all the time. The girl had almost given up and sold the pony, but she'd started having lessons with him. Instead of concentrating on competitions, she'd taken her time to get to know him and build her own riding skills to be able to manage him better.

Amber related to the girl's story as it was so like her own. And there were lots of others like it. She'd been up half the night reading them all. And even her friend, Emily's new pony, Pink, had arrived with a bolting habit. Emily hadn't made any fuss about it at all; she'd just dealt with it quietly and positively: as soon as Pink began one of her accelerations that would take her from walk straight into a flat out gallop, Emily used one of her reins to yank the pony around into a tight circle, which she kept her on until she gave up and went back to walk. Pink had all but given up on her trick now, knowing that this rider wouldn't allow it, and they were building a great relationship.

Amber had lost faith in Molly as the scary moments they'd had together had battered her confidence. Hearing Caroline talk about Lady though, and seeing how other people ended up with such a special bond with their pony after overcoming problems, strengthened her resolve to keep trying.

"Come on girl," she spoke gently to Molly after bridling her and smoothing her forelock. "Let's go for a nice ride." She led her out of the stable towards the mounting block where her parents were waiting with the Fell ponies.

They soon reached the bumpy, pot-holed track that led to the entrance of the forestry. As they headed towards the gate, Amber's mouth became a desert and her heartbeat pounded in her ears.

The gate came into view. It was closed. Horse riders still tried to leave it open, using a large rock to prop it back toward the hedgerow, but walkers often closed it. Now that it had a spring-loaded closing device fitted to it, it was impossible to open without dismounting. This was where Amber should have been kicking her feet out of the stirrups and telling her mum not to get off Pearl as she would do the gate. But Amber was frozen. She didn't move. No words came. The thought of getting back on Molly with no-one to hold her and no mounting block, paralysed her. Her eyes stung and her throat burned at her failure to even attempt the mission she had set herself.

Oblivious to her daughter's distress, Mrs Anderson hopped off Pearl and quickly opened the gate for them all to pass through. She remounted easily while Pearl stood rock-solid, chewing on a mouthful of grass she'd cheekily snatched while her rider had been distracted by the gate.

Amber pushed Molly to the front so that her parents would ride behind her and not see her face. She needed time to compose herself so they wouldn't see how upset she was. She listened to them chat for a while about boring adult stuff like when the car's MOT was due, Mrs Anderson's upcoming dentist appointment and what shopping they needed for the week ahead, until there was silence behind her.

"Amber?"

It seemed she had been asked a question and the silence was waiting for her answer.

"Sorry, what?" Amber sniffed and turned in the saddle.

"I said, the Tetrathlon is coming up soon. The weekend after next. You looking forward to it after all the training you've put in?" her father asked her.

"Er, yeah," Amber replied before quickly turning back to face Molly's pricked chestnut ears. She took a deep breath, inhaling the clean pine scent of the forest that always reminded her of Christmas. *Should I tell them now?* she wondered. *But how? What do I say?*

As if reading her mind, her mother unintentionally provided her with the perfect opportunity. "If it was me, I wouldn't be looking forward to the running or the swimming, they'll be hard work, but at least you know you should do well on the cross-country now that you've been round it with Molly. She was good at the ditch and now that she's seen the water jump, I'm sure she'll understand what to do this time."

"Well... actually... " Amber slowed Molly down and let her parents catch up so that they rode knee to knee

18

on the forestry track. "I'm… er… I'm not riding Molly in the Tetrathlon. I can't. I'm taking Honey."

"What do you mean, you can't?" her mother asked, puzzled by Amber's unexpected announcement.

Now that the time had come, the pent up words tumbled out of Amber like an avalanche. She told them about the gate and the slip rail and how frightened she was about the prospect of trying to manage both obstacles on Molly, especially remounting after the slip rail when Molly would be excited and might be able to see other ponies on the course that she'd want to go after.

"So, I'm sorry, but I just can't do it." By the time she reached the end of her dramatic monologue, she was out of breath due to the ball of tears in her throat that was choking her. "I can't," she whispered.

"Doll, what are you saying you're sorry for?" Mrs Anderson asked. "You have nothing to be sorry about."

Amber couldn't reply, so her mother continued.

"You need to remember this is your hobby – *our* hobby. It's what we do for fun. There's no pressure for you to do anything that makes you feel frightened, Amber. We don't want that. If you want to ride Honey, it's fine, no problem."

Her mother's kindness made Amber's windpipe close up even more. Relief swept through her but it was closely followed by a tide of self-loathing. Her mum was being nice, but she must still be disappointed that her daughter was such a wet lettuce, surely.

"And if you're still not happy with Molly, Love, maybe we should sell her, as we thought. You can just go back to having fun with Honey," her dad joined in, giving Honey a loving pat as he spoke.

"No!" The word sprang from Amber's mouth more harshly than she'd intended. "No," she said again more softly. "Things *are* better with Molly now than they were. I… I just need more time. I… *please* don't sell her," she pleaded.

"Okay. Of course." Mr Anderson shook his head, struggling to understand his daughter's reluctance to part with a pony that repeatedly made her miserable. "You can take your time with Molly. There's no rush."

They rode in silence, each lost in their own thoughts, the ponies' hooves on the track the only sound. Eventually, Mrs Anderson's voice broke the peace. "Remember Amber, it was you who chose to join the

Pony Club and start competing. We're not forcing you to do this. You *can* stop if you like."

As they splashed through streams and cantered through the bracken on the fell, Amber considered her mother's words. Did she want to compete? She thought about the crushing nerves she endured frequently at competitions, and some of the disappointments and disasters she'd experienced. But she also recalled the exhilaration of riding cross-country, of jumping clear, of feeling at one with her pony, the sense of them being a team, and knew that she couldn't give it up. Yes, there were bad parts, but the highs were so high, they made it worth it.

As they re-entered the forest on the way home, the ponies were keen to canter up the forestry hill. Despite being out for nearly two hours, none of them were tired and the Andersons granted their wish. Molly went straight into the lead without even trying, her long hard legs eating up the track ahead of her. As usual she reached the top well before the Fellies so Amber patted her and let her nibble some grass at the side of the track while she waited for her parents to come trotting up the hill on Honey and Pearl.

They rode back towards the farm smiling and chatting easily; the earlier tense atmosphere had vanished like mist.

"I don't want to give up competing," Amber announced when a conversation about whether breaded or battered fish fingers were better had ended. "And I don't want to sell Molly. I still want to compete her, but just not in the Tetrathlon because of the gate and the slip rail. I can still do other stuff like One Day Events and Hunter Trials on her, but for the Tetrathlon, it will have to be Honey."

"Okay Love. That sounds like a good plan," Mrs Anderson agreed happily.

"But… there's just one problem."

"What?" Mr Anderson asked warily.

"I don't actually know if Honey can jump a ninety centimetre course.

- Four -

Equations

Mr Mallard was droning on about factorising quadratic equations, but Amber wasn't listening. She'd zoned out almost immediately. Despite being in set two for maths, it was like a foreign language to her; even worse, as she could grasp French and German but the language of maths was indecipherable to her. She sat next to Sarah, her best friend at school, right at the back of the room. Sarah was in the same boat as Amber when it came to completing the lesson's work, but she was very good at getting George and Dylan, who sat in front of them, to tell them the answers.

Today, Amber found it even harder to listen than normal. She had other things on her mind.

She tried to get comfortable on the hard plastic chair but she was stiff and her muscles ached. Friday night had been the penultimate swimming session at the pool. JoJo had still never turned up to a single training session, but the rest of her teammates, and some senior girls, had been going every week. Thinking about it brought the smell of chlorine to mind, and she rubbed her eyes, remembering the pressure of the goggles as they sucked into her skin. They did less practising of sprint swims now, and more timed episodes, to see how far they could swim in the allotted three minutes of the competition. Amber could do four quick lengths in front crawl, but the effort she put into those drained her completely. After the fourth, she had to flip onto her back and finish off in backstroke. She could usually manage six to six and a half lengths before the whistle blew.

Surprisingly, Emily, who had started poorly in the sprints, did much better when swimming for the full time. She wasn't fast, but she could maintain her pace without fading away like Amber did. She was regularly completing seven lengths, making it look like Amber was going to be the weakest of her team in the swimming phase, much to her disappointment.

The next morning, Saturday, had been their last proper running session. Mr Pryde said they were only going to jog next Saturday, since it would be the day before the Tetrathlon and he didn't wanted to risk anyone injuring themselves on the eve of the competition. But on the Saturday just gone, he'd pushed them hard. Amber continued to ignore his commands that the girls must set off at a sprint and run as hard as they could, for as long as they could. She couldn't run like that, so she continued to do her own thing, setting off steadily, building her speed gradually, until she finished like a steam train, running ram-rod straight with her head up and chest out. Mr Pryde had given up trying to get Amber to run his way, as he'd seen for himself that his method didn't work for her. Amber consistently now finished third out of all of the girls, including some of the seniors. She had never managed to catch her teammate, Chelsea, or the best of the senior girls, Elise, but she wasn't far behind them. On Saturday she'd given everything she had to beat Chelsea, but the other girl could pretty much sprint the full 1,500 metres and didn't tire at the end. Amber just couldn't keep up with her relentless pace. But despite this, she still felt confident that in this phase, she wouldn't let her team down.

Her real worry was still the riding phase. Yesterday, wanting to try Honey over some bigger fences, they'd hired a cross-country course near Penrith which had fences of all sizes and types to help riders prepare their horses for what they might face in competitions. Amber had considered asking her teammates if they'd like to join her, but guiltily dismissed the idea. She still hadn't told them about her plan to ride Honey.

On board Honey again, Amber felt so safe and relaxed, it made her almost giddy. As she warmed Honey up over some of the smaller fences, the knots of nerves in her stomach untied themselves and she laughed with pleasure as they splashed through the water jump, popped over a ditch and even tackled their first corner fence, which Honey jumped without the slightest hesitation.

But when her father called her to try some of the larger fences, like those Honey would need to take on at the Tetrathlon the following weekend, Amber's heart sank. Compared to Molly, she could feel Honey's lack of power. What Molly could jump easily would be a huge effort for Honey. Could she make it round a full course?

"Try these." Mr Anderson selected a cluster of larger, but straightforward fences for Amber to start with: a roll-top, a hanging log, a palisade and a skinny topped with brush. Honey hopped over all of them happily and went on to clear an arrowhead, a chair, a barrel fence styled to look like a train, and a steeplechase fence. But by the time she'd done all of those, and her father was pointing to a large, square box fence, Amber could feel that Honey was spent. She'd had to use more energy to jump the bigger fences and she was starting to feel flat. Amber didn't want to put the brave little pony at any more fences in case she tried to jump them but was too tired to clear them and hurt herself on the solid and unforgiving obstacles.

Loading Honey back into the trailer at the end of the session, Amber was pleased. Honey had the heart of a lion and had not refused any of the fences she'd been presented at. That gave Amber some confidence for the weekend ahead, but there was still the question of Honey's stamina. She got tired jumping a full course of eighty-centimetre jumps, especially when there were plenty of hills, which there were on the Brantfort course. Would she be able to get round? Would her courage compensate for what she lacked in power? Was she capable of clearing the dreaded wall? Molly had got Amber over that at the recent One Day Event by sheer athleticism, when Amber's fear of the fence made her ride it dreadfully. Honey wouldn't be able to do that. Amber would need to commit to the fence; she'd need to see a stride and push for it. *Can I do that?* she wondered. *I trust Honey, but is the fence too big for her? What if she tries to take it on and hits it? She could really hurt herself.*

Amber's doubts relayed through her mind in a never-ending loop. She was imagining poor Honey hitting the top of the wall, and tipping over in a rotational fall when she felt Sarah nudging her in the ribs. Her friend had been doodling a love heart in the back of her maths book with the initials H.D. inside, but had abandoned it and flipped to the front as Mr Mallard was instructing them to open their textbooks and work through the equations on page forty-six.

"I expect you to get at least the first five done by the end of the lesson," he instructed while writing the date on the whiteboard. "If not, it will be your homework. Off you go." The teacher went to sit at his desk to check something on his computer.

Amber opened the textbook on the desk to page 46 and looked at the numbers and letters on it. It might as well have been hieroglyphics. She pulled a face and turned to Sarah, who was also looking at the page with her nose wrinkled in disgust. The two girls looked at each other blankly. Sarah giggled and pushed her ruler into the back of the blond boy who sat at the desk in front of her. "Dy-lan?" she whispered flirtatiously.

The boy turned around and winked. "Can I help you?" he smiled knowingly. But before Sarah had a chance to speak again, Mr Mallard's voice boomed, "Dylan Wright! Turn around! Everyone get on in silence please!"

Amber sighed and slumped in her chair. She was going to have homework that night. She went back to trying to balance the pony equation in her head. At the moment, that was far more important.

- Five -

Quiet as a Mouse

The week dragged by, but soon it was Friday and time for the last swimming session before the branch Tetrathlon on Sunday. Amber could already feel the nerves stirring inside her, yawning and stretching, limbering up for a long weekend.

Emily must have been feeling the same as she was unusually subdued. Her mood certainly didn't match her sunshine yellow swimming costume. Chelsea alone seemed to be unaffected and chattered away as the girls got changed. Amber only gave her half an ear as she kept talking about people she didn't know, but she tuned in again when she heard a name she recognised: Elisha Templeton.

"Heard from the Taylor-Tillman's that Elisha Templeton has a new horse. I think her usual one, Thunder Cat, has picked up an injury so he's having to have a break to recover. They sold her pony, North Quest, last winter so she's got another – the same breeder as Thunder Cat. Probably cost a fortune, knowing them." Chelsea rammed her socks into her trainers and placed them in a locker before unzipping her sports jacket and putting it in on top.

"What's this one called?" Amber asked, unable to feign indifference. Although she detested Elisha for her arrogance and the way she treated both people and horses, she had a morbid fascination with wanting to know what she was up to.

"Erm… hang on." Chelsea consulted her phone before turning it to show Amber and Emily the screen. On it was a Horse & Hound article showing a smug looking Elisha astride a tall iron grey with a glossy black mane. The headline read *Templeton a Danger to her Competitors with New Mount*. Amber quickly scanned the article which explained how Elisha had been one of the top twenty riders in the Young Rider British Show jumping Winter League on Thunder Cat and was already off to a good start in the Summer League on her new ride.

"*Danger Mouse*?" Amber exclaimed as she reached the part of the article about Elisha's new mount. "What kind of name is that for a horse?"

"It's a cartoon character from the eighties, like Thunder Cat," Emily said. "I've heard it's the breeder's thing. They name all their horses after cartoon characters. Others I've heard of are Battle Cat, Top Cat, Super Ted... and Mighty Mouse."

Amber harrumphed, pushing her clothes into a locker and pinning the key onto her costume. "I wonder how Natalie's getting on," she said, more to herself than anyone else. She hadn't seen many posts on Instagram from the girl she'd met just over a year ago. She'd gone from a timid, novice rider to a serious competitor in what seemed like the blink of an eye, since she'd sold the pony she'd been completely unsuited to, and bought an experienced competition pony from Elisha.

"Oh, you mean Natalie Riley? She's got a new one too. Groove Jet. Not sure if it's on loan or lease. It belongs to the Coles but Amelia's grown out of him and moved onto horses, and Patrick is still on his 12.2hh. They want to keep Jet for Patrick when he's grown a bit and is ready for a bigger pony, so in the meantime they've asked Natalie to ride him and keep him going until they want him back. He's not an easy ride though, from what I hear. I think Natalie will have her work cut out."

"Hmm." That was exactly what Amber herself had said when Natalie bought Rocky from Elisha, but the pair had quickly clicked and apart from some problems at the first Pony Club camp she'd taken him to, Natalie had been on a path lined with gold ever since. Maybe she could do it again with another 'difficult' pony. Amber didn't know whether she hoped so or not.

She was surprised that Emily hadn't known about Natalie's new pony. She was one of those people who seemed to know everyone and everything, or at least, could find out through someone's friend of a friend. Being a social butterfly meant that Emily was well connected and usually a font of all knowledge when it came to the lives of people she knew. She appeared to be off-the-ball at the moment and Amber wondered if something was troubling her beyond nerves about the Tetrathlon.

The time in the pool was spent fairly leisurely. Mr Pryde didn't appear for a while, which was most unlike him. He was usually there in his flip flops right from the beginning, blowing his whistle and shouting commands, but that evening there was no sign of him. Amber knew he must be about since he'd clearly brought Emily, but didn't concern herself with asking about him. She just set herself the challenge of doing as many continuous lengths as she could without pausing. The other girls seemed to be doing the same.

Towards the end of the hour, Mr Pryde showed up and made them do one final timed swim before the real thing on Sunday. Normally, Amber busted a gut to do her very best, but she was distracted by seeing how uncharacteristically tired Mr Pryde looked. He was never tired. He was like the Duracell bunny every other time she'd seen him. That, combined with the fact that Emily had been quiet earlier, preoccupied Amber and she swam just under six lengths by the time the whistle sounded to signal that time was up. Strangely, Mr Pryde made no comment on her performance.

As the girls climbed, dripping from the pool to head back to the changing rooms, Mr Pryde stopped them briefly. His normally square shoulders drooped as he spoke. "Well done girls. I think you're all ready to do your best. I'll see you at the pool on Sunday morning. Er… there'll be no running tomorrow morning. I think it's best if you have a day off, eat plenty of carbs and get an early night. See you on Sunday."

"Is your dad alright?" Amber asked Emily as they towelled their hair back in the changing room. "He doesn't seem himself today." Nor do you, she thought to herself, but didn't say so out loud.

"Yeah, he's fine." Emily responded, rather evasively. Obviously that was her way of shutting the conversation down and showing that she didn't want to discuss it. Amber didn't push the issue.

As usual, Chelsea was the first to get changed and be ready to leave.

"Right, you two. I'm off. See you on Sunday, ready to kick some butt!" She used her backside to nudge the locker door closed, just as she said 'butt'. Amber giggled but Emily didn't react. "I think we'll do well." Chelsea continued. "We've trained hard and we've got four good ponies ready to do their part too. See ya!" She saluted and strode away from them, the changing room door whacking against the wall as usual; Chelsea always used more force than was necessary to open the door. "Ooops!" she said, before disappearing.

Now would've been the time to ask Emily if she was alright, but Amber was lost in Chelsea's final words: 'we've got four good ponies ready to do their part'.

Yes, we have, she thought to herself, *but one of them isn't the one you're thinking of.* Amber had chickened out of telling her teammates about her decision to ride Honey instead of Molly on Sunday. She hadn't even told JoJo. *How will they react when they see me on Honey?*

She didn't have long to wait to find out.

- Six -

Bad Dreams

The day of the Tetrathlon dawned bright and warm with a spirited chorus from the cheerful birds. But the birds' joy at the start of the new day failed to fortify Amber. She was worn out from the vivid dreams she'd had the night before. She had that strange sensation of not quite knowing which parts had actually happened and which parts her brain had made up to trick and worry her. On top of that, the nausea that always accompanied her on competition days was present as usual, but today it was even worse; as if she'd just stepped off a waltzer. She hadn't been able to eat any breakfast. Her mother had presented her with bacon and eggs to 'keep you going,' but just the smell of it turned her stomach. Now she was at the barn at Brantfort Bridge that was being used for the shooting phase and she was shaking. How she was going to hold the gun steady enough to shoot straight was beyond her.

The team members had been given a running order for the day: Chelsea would be first to go and would compete against the other teams' number 1 competitor. Then Emily would be second, followed by Amber, with JoJo going last. Helpfully, there were three other junior girls' teams so only four heats were needed.

Chelsea had already shot her target and been whisked off to the swimming pool that had been hired for the competition. Emily was currently shooting hers and Amber stood behind the barrier watching. The organisers had set up proper turning targets and Amber observed nervously as they turned to face the shooter before quickly twisting away to hide the result of the shot. She tried to concentrate on her breathing to calm herself and shoved her hands into her armpits to try to stop them trembling. She'd have appreciated some pockets to hide her hands in, but her Pony Club sweatshirt didn't have any. Instead of concentrating on watching the teams' number two doing their shoot, Amber's mind wandered back to the previous day. After a lesson with Caroline on Molly, followed by cleaning all Honey's tack, the Andersons had headed to Brantfort Bridge to walk the cross-country course. They'd arranged to meet the Jones' there so that JoJo could walk her course with Amber. Mrs Jones would need to go with Matthew to guide him round his minimus track, which was shorter and didn't follow the same route as the juniors' course.

"Right, off you go!" JoJo shooed her mother and brother away as soon as the Andersons climbed out of their car, letting Kasper the cocker spaniel out for a run around. He was meant to be accompanying them on their course walk, but as usual he'd come out of the car like a balloon that had been blown up and released. He'd gone whizzing off somewhere and would soon be lost. He was a liability.

"You seem keen to get rid of poor Matthew," Amber joked as they walked towards a laminated poster that had been pinned to a tree in the area they were expecting to see the cross-country warm-up.

"No, it's Mum actually. She's doing my head in"

"Oh? Why?"

"Aww, nothing." JoJo peered intently at the poster and changed the subject. "Look, it says they're running the course in the opposite direction to the One Day Event. And they've moved the start too."

Mrs Jones had clearly realised the same thing as she and Matthew were getting back into their car and driving slowly across the bumpy field to the relocated start. The Andersons attempted to do the same thing, but first they had to find Kasper. This proved to be an impossible task, despite all four of them shouting his name in all directions.

"Oh, that damn dog!" Mr Anderson, usually so laid back, looked like he was about to blow a fuse. "We'll just have to look for him on the way round. Come on."

They all piled back into the car and followed the tracks of flattened grass left by others who had clearly done the same thing.

They parked amongst the other cars which were arranged haphazardly around the caravan where the scorers would sit tomorrow. The girls went to take a look at the map of the course pinned to the side of it while Amber's parents set off to search for Kasper. There were twenty obstacles, including the gate and slip rail to be opened, with an optimum time based on a speed of 450 metres per second. This meant nothing to Amber as she knew that with Honey, she would inevitably be over the time. She would just have to go at Honey's pace, accepting that they would get faults.

JoJo interrupted her thoughts. "It's a long course but it won't trouble ours. Molly and Merry will get round well inside the time." Amber flinched at her words. She was going to have to tell JoJo. She couldn't say nothing and then appear on Honey tomorrow. What would her friend think of her if she did that? *But how can I tell her?*

Amber trailed behind JoJo as she strode off towards the first fence. *Should I make something up and say Molly's gone lame so that's why I'm having to ride Honey?* The lie was so tempting. And it would be so easy. Ponies went lame all the time, and Amber never lied, so JoJo would probably accept it. It was the perfect escape from having to reveal the real reason. Amber knew that JoJo would be disappointed for the team. She was ultra-competitive and this event had been her main focus for months. But more than that, Amber worried that her friend would be disappointed in her. JoJo, who was good at everything, and seemed to fear nothing, couldn't possibly understand how Amber felt. Although Amber was the older of the two, she looked up to JoJo and aspired to be like her. She couldn't bear to have her look at her with pity... or worse... disdain. But she knew she couldn't lie.

Amber remained silent as they began to walk the course. She was rehearsing possible ways to introduce her confession, weighing up the pros and cons of different approaches. JoJo was commenting on the fences, most of which were the same as the recent One Day Event. However, due to the reversal of the course, the ski jump couldn't be used so it had been replaced with a double of off-set houses. JoJo was talking about the best way to approach this fence on a forward going pony who might not see the angled second element and gallop straight past it, but Amber wasn't listening. Her parents, up ahead, were still calling for Kasper, but Amber couldn't join in. She was acutely focused on finding the words... the right words that would spare her humiliation.

Then they reached the slip rail.

The dreaded obstacle was number eight on the course, right after the ditch and rails. It was situated in the trees next to the log pile, the highest point of the course, from where everything else could be seen: the collecting ring where ponies would be warming up, the start, a good proportion of the course, and the finish. Amber breathed a sigh of relief. She'd made the right decision. If she'd been riding Molly, it would've been a disaster. The pony, with her blood up and adrenaline fizzing through her veins, would never have stood still to be remounted here, where she could see everything going on.

JoJo heard Amber's sigh and misread it for anxiety. She put her hand on Amber's shoulder. "Right, I think you'll need to make sure Molly isn't looking over towards the start when you go to remount," she said, reading Amber's mind. "You should turn her around, face her away from home and use the log pile as a mounting block. Don't let her see other ponies and hopefully you'll be able to get back on quick before she moves."

Amber was touched by JoJo's awareness of her concern and she gulped before blurting out her carefully rehearsed words. Except they didn't come out as planned.

"Not riding Molly… Honey… can't… sorry, but… er, yeah."

"Sorry, what are you saying?" JoJo asked.

"I'm riding Honey tomorrow," Amber whispered, looking at her feet.

JoJo stared at her for several moments. Amber bowed her head even further, waiting for the weight of JoJo's displeasure to settle upon her.

"Why?" she asked, clearly shocked. "Just because of the slip rail?"

Just because of the slip rail. JoJo didn't need to say it, but that sentence told Amber exactly what she was thinking: that Amber was a baby, a scaredy-cat, a wimp.

"Mmm hmm." She couldn't speak. Couldn't even look up.

"Oh. Well, that's… right. Okay."

Amber could tell that JoJo had been about to say something else. Probably 'that's disappointing,' or 'that's stupid,' then she'd bitten her tongue. But although she hadn't said the words, Amber could read them on JoJo's face.

They continued in near silence, only remarking on the new fence that was replacing the tyre jump: a keyhole fence built between two trees. The actual jump was an imposing upright brush but brush also dangled from a canopy above the fence, meaning that riders would need to make sure they were well forward to avoid whacking their faces on it as they passed through. "Interesting," was all JoJo said.

"Yeah," Amber agreed, shakily, not wanting to show that this fence was going to keep her awake all night.

By the time they completed the course and caught up to her parents, Amber noting with regret that the enormous and dreaded wall was the final fence, Kasper still hadn't reappeared. They distracted themselves from not speaking by joining in calling for the lost dog. There was still no sign of him and Amber's parents were starting to get concerned, until they heard an odd sound.

It stopped them all in their tracks as it floated towards them: a plaintive keening coming from the direction of the cars. They hurried towards the sound, anxious about what they would find. The sorrowful wailing increased in volume as they approached their car. They were briefly aware of Mrs Jones and Matthew, who had already returned to theirs after their shorter course walk, pointing and laughing, but they hurried past them, keen to see what was making such a desolate cry.

A small golden dog lay beside the Anderson's car. Kasper! His eyes were closed, his nose pointed towards the clouds. Oblivious to all around him, he lay there, lost in his own world, howling with such determined misery, it made everyone break into fits of giggles. Kasper was so committed to his despair he didn't notice them at first.

"He's been doing that since we got back!" Matthew told them. "We called to him but he didn't seem to hear us, just kept his eyes closed and carried on howling. He thinks he's a wolf!"

"I think he's enjoying feeling sorry for himself," Mrs Jones smiled. "Right, come on then you two. We'd better get home and sort everything out for tomorrow. Matthew, have you found your swimming trunks yet?"

The Jones' drove away while the Andersons snapped Kasper out of his woeful trance. He'd clearly convinced himself that he'd never see his family again as his reaction to being reunited with them was so over-the-top, it even managed to make Amber smile. But once she was in the back in the car by herself, her mind carried her back to JoJo's reaction to the news she'd be riding Honey tomorrow, and the fact that she'd barely spoken to Amber for the rest of the course walk.

Had they fallen out? Amber wasn't sure. The thought settled itself in and got comfortable, ready to torment her all night.

– Seven –

Sink or Swim

"Okay. Number twos, your shoot is complete. Number threes, please step forward."

Amber was brought back into the present with the steward's announcement that it was her turn to shoot. She blinked and refocused her eyes on the scene ahead of her. Stewards were taking down the targets the number twos had just shot and replacing them with new ones for the next competitors. Mr Pryde was packing up Emily's gun as he'd been her loader and Emily was waving at Amber.

Mr Jones suddenly appeared behind her and ushered her forward towards the bench.

"Good luck!" her parents chorused as she walked away from them.

"I've no idea how that went." Emily looked paler than usual, suggesting that she was suffering from nerves too. "But on to the swimming now." Amber expected her to pull a face or something to show how little she was looking forward to the swimming phase, but her expression remained neutral as Mr Pryde came up beside her.

"Come on then, Em, let's get you to the pool." He nodded at Mr Jones and wished Amber luck with her shoot. Then they were away, leaving Amber trembling in front of the target. It was currently facing her, staring her down, intimidating her.

"Okay competitors. You should be your team's number three. Please check you're in the right line. Blakefield Pony Club, you should be shooting at target one. Brantfort, you're target two. Copton Hunt, you're target three and West Hall Farmers, you are target four."

Amber noted the other three girls lined up with her. She was in the right place, but the girls in lanes three and four swapped.

"If everyone is ready, load and stand by for practice shots to begin."

Mr Jones pushed a pellet into the pistol he held and placed it on the bench in front of him. Amber took her glasses out of their case and put them on. "Remember to breathe… and count," he whispered to Amber. "You've got four seconds, so don't rush."

The other three girls were all shooting with their right hands, but Amber turned her left shoulder towards the target, ready to aim when instructed. Although she was right-handed, she'd been forced to learn to shoot left-handed when she'd broken her right collarbone seven months ago. As a result, the strength of grip in her left hand was now superior to her right. She had tried, in the Jones' garage, to shoot right-handed, but it felt odd and she couldn't close her left eye, meaning she had to wear an eye patch. She'd decided to continue shooting left-handed.

"Are you ready?" A steward called. Amber gripped the gun tightly. "Stand by. Fire."

Amber hurriedly raised her left arm and squinted through the gun's sights. She completely forgot to count and shakily pulled the trigger as soon as she thought she was aiming at the bullseye. She lowered her gun well before the other girls in her heat.

"Reload."

"Slow down," Mr Jones whispered to her again as he reloaded. "Use the time. You're rushing." He passed the gun back to her and she took some deep, shaky breaths in an attempt to steady herself.

Amber's next two shots weren't great. She pressed the trigger too firmly, making the gun jerk upwards as the pellet was released. Mr Jones whispered "four" and then "six" to let Amber know where her shots landed. By the time she'd completed her final two practice shots, she'd calmed down. With a better feel for the timings, she settled into a rhythm. Amber blocked out everything in her mind and around her and focused on lining up the sights with the bullseye like a bird of prey.

Soon it was time for the real thing. Amber rolled her shoulders to release the tension as the targets were changed and turned away. For the real thing, they would be firing at turning targets.

The command was given to load. "Are you ready?" Amber took a deep breath and held it. "Watch and shoot."

The targets turned to face the shooters.

By the time she finished, Mr Jones had whispered "eight" four times and "ten" three times. There were a few shots he wasn't sure of; he hadn't seen where they'd landed before the target turned away.

"Well done," Mr Jones smiled. "I was worried there for a minute but you got it together. Impressive composure."

"Number threes, your shoot is complete. Can the final competitors please step forward?"

"Thanks," Amber mumbled as she turned away from Mr Jones, coming face to face with JoJo who was approaching the bench for her turn. "Hi," Amber ventured, uncertainly.

"Hi," JoJo said, walking past Amber to take up her position next to her father.

"I'll… I'll see you at the pool then."

JoJo cast a glance in her direction and nodded before turning away again. Amber stared at the back of her friend's head and noticed that, despite the early hour, JoJo's blonde hair was perfectly presented in a reverse braid topped with a messy top knot. *How on earth can she have managed to do that by this time of morning?* Amber thought to herself. *Even if I had all day, I couldn't get my hair to look like that.*

Amber was completely distracted by JoJo's hair all the way to the swimming pool. She knew that if she ever managed to get her hair looking that good, she'd want to leave it like that for a week, if she could, to make the most of it. She'd even be prepared to sleep in a sitting position to avoid messing it up. But there was JoJo, who was going to be swimming and riding; her hairdo could not survive those two activities, yet she'd still bothered to do it.

Lost in her thoughts, Amber didn't even realise that they'd pulled into the car park of the swimming pool, or that her father wasn't in the car with them.

"Where's Dad?" she asked, slightly panicked.

"Where's Dad? Amber, have you been on another planet? You know where Dad is," her mother replied, exasperation lacing her voice. Amber looked at her mother in the interior mirror, raising her eyebrows in a question. She couldn't believe she'd sat in the back of the car even though the front passenger seat was empty.

"He's gone with Lou to the farm. He's getting Honey ready to bring her to the field for the cross-country after lunch. Lou is doing the same with Jo and Matthew's ponies so we'll meet them there after you've swum.

"JoJo." Amber corrected her mum.

"What?"

"Jo… oh never mind." Amber climbed out of the car, dragging her kit bag with her. Her stomach growled so loudly, even Mrs Anderson heard it. Amber was beginning to regret having no breakfast.

"Here, eat this," her mother said, reading her mind and handing her a banana. "You need something in that stomach to get you through the swimming."

The chewy texture of the banana in her mouth made Amber feel like she might puke, but she forced it down, knowing that her mother was right. She'd need some energy to make it through three minutes of hard swimming. She just wished it could have been a chocolate bar instead.

Leaving Mrs Anderson at the viewing area, Amber headed into the changing rooms where she bumped straight into Chelsea who was dressed and drying her hair after completing her swim.

"Hi. How'd your swim go?" asked Amber.

Chelsea switched off the hairdryer and pulled her still slightly damp tawny hair into a bobble, not even looking in the mirror to see what it looked like. The fact that it was full of lumps and bumps reassured Amber.

"Great. Well, I think so. I did just over eight lengths. Emily's swimming now. I'm going to nip through and see if I can catch the end of it. And I'll stay to watch yours. Good luck."

"Yeah, well done. Thanks," Amber replied, wincing as the door whacked the wall as it always did when Chelsea opened it.

"Ooops!" she said, as she always did. It seemed that the swim hadn't sapped any of Chelsea's strength.

Amber was left alone in the changing room. As she pulled off her clothes and placed them in a locker, she took a few shaky breaths to steady her nerves. All she had to do was swim. Nothing could go wrong. She'd practised swimming for three minutes many times and knew she could do it. *So why do I feel so awful?*

Was it because she was dreading the riding phase, worrying whether Honey could cope with the full ninety course, and even if she did, how many time penalties she would bring back? Was it because of the gate and slip rail and knowing she had to remount on the course? Was it because JoJo seemed annoyed with her over her decision not to ride Molly today? Or was it because she was dreading being the team's worst swimmer?

Amber had spent so much time worrying about this competition, about being a part of a team and not wanting to let her teammates down, yet it didn't even feel as if they were a team. She'd barely seen or spoken to any of them yet and JoJo had practically snubbed her. She wasn't feeling very inspired.

But it was time.

Clutching her towel around her, Amber noticed that the other three girls in her heat were ready and heading to the showers before making their way to the pool for their swim. Amber shuffled off the bench she was sitting on to follow them.

As the girls reached the showers, the number two swimmers were just coming out. Emily was the last one to leave, but the most noticeable in a bright orange swimsuit piped in black. It made Amber think of a tiger.

"Hey, how was your swim?" Amber asked, pleased to have the chance to speak to her friend.

"Oh, the usual. Just over seven lengths. Dad will be peeved, no doubt, that I didn't manage to get any further than usual, but at least I didn't do worse. He'll have to be happy with that. I don't know how the others did; I was too busy counting my lengths to notice what they were doing."

"It doesn't matter anyway," Amber said. "You weren't in a race with them. It's about our combined scores. Seven is great and Chelsea got over eight. JoJo will be fab too…" she trailed off as the pressure to do well sank into her gut.

"And so will you. I'll try and get changed quickly so I can come and watch." Emily gave her a wet hug.

"Oh no, it's okay. Just take your time." Amber was starting to shiver despite the hot, fuggy atmosphere in the showers.

"As if. I want to be there to holler for you. You might not see me, but you'll deffo hear me!"

Oh no! She thought again as she came out to the poolside. The viewing gallery was packed. She could see her mum, Chelsea and her dad, Emily's mum and Harry, her brother amongst the spectators. The poolside was lined with coaches and officials ready to watch each girl and measure their swim; the long sides of the pool had been marked out in metres. The pool itself had been split into lanes using lane ropes. It was so much different to what she was used to, she felt like a team of synchronised swimmers were doing a high speed, complicated routine in her stomach.

After a brief warm-up, during which each girl's coach gave some last-minute encouragement, the swimmers were called to the deep end to start. All of them climbed out of the pool and stood at the edge, wanting to take advantage of diving in. Once the starter was satisfied that each girl was in the correct lane, and the lane judges were in position, she gave the signal to the time-keeper to get ready to start the stopwatch.

"Take your marks."

The girls were poised like statues, ready to dive.

A whistle blew, slicing through the silence, releasing the girls from their stillness.

Spectators roared as everyone yelled encouragement to their team member but Amber wasn't aware of anything except the sound of water rushing past her ears as she ploughed down her lane in front crawl, swimming as if her life depended on it.

Her lungs and heart were soon screaming at her and, as she completed her fourth length, she flipped over onto her back to continue in backstroke. She could see the other girls in their lanes, but had no idea how she compared to them. Soon, she saw and heard the starter ringing a hand bell from the deep end of the pool to signal they were halfway through their time.

Despite her weariness, Amber kicked harder and pushed on.

In no time, the bell was ringing again, which she knew meant there were only thirty seconds left. The spectators roared again, but the sound was muffled by the water in Amber's ears as she battled on for the final seconds.

A whistle blasted to pronounce the end of the swim. Amber was in the middle of a length when she heard the whistle. Being in the first lane, she reached for the wall on her right and clutched at it while she recovered.

"Whoo-hoo. Go Amber!"

Squinting into the viewing area, Amber could just make out the blurred forms of Emily and Harry clapping in her direction, showing that their applause was aimed at her. She smiled weakly but inside she was defeated. She'd been so determined to equal Emily's seven lengths but she knew she hadn't managed it.

Her legs barely had the energy to get her back to the changing room and, as she stood under the shower, she could scarcely raise her arms to wash the chlorine out of her hair.

As she had with Emily, she bumped into JoJo in the showers as she headed out for her heat. Amber couldn't tell what had happened to her hairdo as it was hidden under a navy-blue swimming cap. JoJo looked like a professional swimmer in her matching navy costume, her long limbs ready to drive her through the water.

Without making eye contact, they exchanged a few tight words of 'how did you do?' and 'good luck' before JoJo disappeared out to the pool area and Amber locked herself into a changing room, where she had to sit, wrapped in her towel for several minutes before she could summon the will to take on the task of getting dressed.

She took so long that she missed JoJo's swim. She didn't need to see it to know it would be brilliant. By the time she got to the viewing gallery, the final swimmers were climbing out of the pool.

"Here she is!" her mother exclaimed. "I was just about to come and look for you. I was worried you'd drowned in the shower or something."

Amber didn't acknowledge the joke. "How did JoJo do?" she asked.

"She was amazing! She swam flat out for the whole three minutes; tumble turns, the lot. She was like an Olympian! She got nearly nine lengths!"

"Oh, that's good," Amber said while thinking how hard she'd worked and how exhausted she'd been just getting her six and a half lengths.

"Yes, I think your team are off to a good start. You've all swum well and Peter said the shoot wasn't bad either, especially you and Jo. Let's go and meet Dad and have some lunch. You need to get your strength back before the riding and the running this afternoon. I'm glad it's you doing this, not me. I'd never make it to the end."

Amber knew her mum was only joking, but her words struck a chord. She'd only ever practised for the Tetrathlon one phase at a time, but today she had to do all of them, one after another. *Can I do it? Can I get to the end?* she worried. The two hardest phases were still to come. Honey would need her to ride strongly all the way round today's mighty course if they were going to complete it, but her energy was spent. She felt like a phone out of battery – she needed to recharge, but there wasn't time. The feeling of nausea she'd started the day with hadn't left her, but now she wasn't sure if it was nerves, disappointment or hunger that was making her feel so sick. She knew she'd have to eat to make it through the day, but the thought of food was so repulsive, her stomach contracted.

I've got to get through this, she thought.

But can you? the voice in her head asked her. *Can you do it? Maybe it's too much for you. Physically, you're not as strong as the others and mentally... well... you're not too great with pressure, are you?*

If everyone else can do it, so can I, Amber snapped defiantly.

But did she believe her own words? Was she strong enough to do this?

The truth was... she didn't know.

The voice had nothing more to add.

– Eight –

Roar

Usually, once mounted on Honey at a competition, the pony's eagerness to get started instilled confidence in Amber and numbed her nerves to a bearable level. But not today.

The Fell pony was alive with anticipation and Amber managed a smile as she stroked the coppery mane while she waited to be allowed into the warm-up area. Currently, only the teams' number one and number two riders were allowed in. The first two competitors had already set off onto the course, Chelsea being the first rider to start.

But just as the third rider was counted down and sent on their way, Amber saw something that made her tremble. Chelsea was riding off the course at a walk.

"Em!" Amber managed to squeak to Emily, who was trying to contain a highly excited Pink in the warm-up area. "Look." Amber used her riding crop to point in the direction of their teammate who was riding, shoulders slumped, back towards them.

Emily wasn't able to reply or find out what had happened as Chelsea rode back through the warm-up area to get to the trailer park. She was too busy trying to get Pink to stop bouncing on the spot and approach the practice fences.

"Chelsea," Amber called, riding to catch the girl up as she dismounted and walked straight past. "What happened?"

Chelsea pulled her pony to a stop and loosened the girth. She didn't look up at Amber as she spoke. "We were fine. I'd done the alternative at the ditch as I knew she wouldn't jump it, but she was going great. Until that new keyhole fence in the trees near the church... " Amber didn't interrupt when Chelsea paused. It was pretty obvious what she was going to say. "Skye hated it. There was no alternative so I had to keep trying, but she just wouldn't do it. It's a pretty dark fence, in the shade of all the trees, and it seems she doesn't like jumping in bad light, so yeah, eliminated."

Amber didn't know what to say. This was so unexpected. Chelsea was the star of the team, besides JoJo. She was the last person Amber expected to be the discount score, but that's how it looked. She was saved from having to console her teammate when a steward started calling for the third riders to come and warm-up.

"I'm so sorry... I've... I've got to go," was all she managed. She received no words of advice or encouragement from Chelsea, who was distracted by her own misfortune. She was so absorbed in her thoughts, she didn't notice that Amber was riding Honey instead of Molly.

Amber was just in time to see Emily being counted down from the start box as she rode into the warm-up area. Pink shot out of the box like an aeroplane ready for take-off, but she soon slowed as she took in the first fence. Amber frowned, wondering what the problem was. The first fence was just a simple sloping rail: a Jacob's Ladder. She rode into the corner of the warm-up area, pulling up her saddle flap to check her girth at the same time as viewing Pink's approach to the first fence. Now she could see what the problem was. When she'd walked the course last night, the fences were flagged and numbered, but now she could see that some of them had been 'dressed'. The innocuous first fence now had two toddler sized carved bears sitting up on their haunches on either side of it, and the next jump, the zig-zag, had bales of straw placed in front of the simple rail to make it a wider obstacle.

Emily rode strongly and managed to get Pink over the first fence, albeit with an awkward cat jump, and they wiggled towards the second fence.

"Come on Honeybun." Amber began warming up. A strange sensation flooded her, making her feel like liquid in the saddle. She pictured herself melting like a candle as her nerves consumed her from within. Now, not only did she have the dreaded new keyhole fence and the awful wall to worry about, would she even make it past the first fence? Normally, a single dandelion minding its own business in the grass verge was enough to make Honey bring out her praying mantis impression. How was she going to react when she saw two bears waiting to pounce on her?

As if to illustrate her fears, the last of the number two riders was eliminated at the bear fence and had to leave the course without even getting started.

"Okay, number threes stand by," the collecting ring steward called. "Amber Anderson… two minutes."

Amber gave Honey one last pop over the practice fence then let her rest. She didn't want her to be tired before they began. She saw her parents waving at her as they walked up the slope that would take them to the highest point of the course from where they could see a lot of the fences. She gave a little wave back, but was stilled as her name was called.

"Amber Anderson to the start please."

Her lips stuck to her teeth as she gasped. It was like being called to step forward for the guillotine rather than a fun activity she'd volunteered for. Now it mattered. With Chelsea eliminated, she needed to be the team member whose score could be dropped. Amber had to get round the cross-country. The pressure was so tangible she could feel its weight pressing down on her, threatening to crush her spirit.

As she circled the start box, having been told she had a minute to wait by the starter, Amber noticed that

JoJo had entered the warm-up area on Merry. At lunchtime, the team members and their parents had all sat together to discuss the day so far and the phases still to come. Mr Pryde had been very enthusiastic in his advice about how the girls should ride the cross-country course, even though he didn't ride himself. Emily had eye-rolled and tutted quietly throughout, making Amber smirk, enjoying their shared joke. She'd tried to include JoJo, but hadn't been able to make eye contact with her as she hadn't looked her way even once. Ever since she'd told JoJo she was riding Honey, not Molly, in the Tetrathlon, it seemed as if her friend was snubbing her. It increased the burden on Amber to justify her decision and win back JoJo's approval.

"Thirty seconds," the starter called. "I'll count you down from ten."

The small amount of sandwich Amber had managed to force down at lunchtime threatened to reappear as she rode Honey into the start box. Some ponies wouldn't stand quietly in the box and had to run through it once they'd been told to go, but Honey was quite happy to stand and wait. Amber also thought it would give her time to work out that the bears were just wood and wouldn't kill her if she had time to see them first.

"Ten... nine..." Her countdown started. Instinctively, she tightened her grip on the reins and leaned forward. Feeling her rider's changing position, Honey's ears flicked forward and back, waiting for the signal to move. "Three... two ... one ... go! Good luck!" the starter called.

And they were off. Honey immediately clocked the bears and baulked, trying to back away from the fence. Amber, who'd been like jelly on a plate only moments before was now fuelled with determination and rode strongly.

"GO ON," she roared. It worked. Honey was so surprised to hear the fierceness in her rider's voice, she shot forward and over the fence. She still kept a suspicious eye on the silent statues on either side of her, but was invested with Amber's conviction, making her brave.

"Good girl!" Amber patted the mare encouragingly as they headed for the straw bales. This held no problem for Honey as they'd often practised over straw bales at the farm and at JoJo's.

Soon the gate, the palisade and the skinny log were behind them. Next was the double of off-set houses. This posed no problem to Honey as she jumped the first house neatly and Amber had plenty of time to turn and straighten her for the next, angled house. Then it was up the slope to the ditch and rails. The hill sapped some of Honey's energy and the rails were higher than they were used to. Amber pushed her into a strong canter and they sailed through the three elements. Honey didn't give the bogey ditch a second glance.

And then it was time for the cause of Amber's nightmares: the slip rail. It was located in a small cluster of trees beside the church, next to the log pile which wasn't being used. Amber kicked her feet out of the stirrups and slid off Honey as they approached it. She managed the top rail easily, leading Honey obediently over the lower rail. Having returned the top rail to its position, Amber prepared to remount, deciding to use the handily placed log pile as a mounting block. Her left leg wobbled as she placed her foot in the stirrup and swung herself hurriedly back into the saddle, but she needn't have worried. Honey remained perfectly still, pleased to have an opportunity to get her breath back.

"Right lass, let's go." Amber pushed Honey back into a canter and headed for the chair fence, now adorned with boxes of colourful pansies. Amber rode strongly, remembering Honey's aversion to flowers. The pony lowered her head to look, but sensing her rider's determination, she jumped the fence strongly.

They pressed on towards the next clump of trees around the back of the church, where the dreaded keyhole fence lurked in its shadow. It looked huge as Amber approached it and she realised that Chelsea was right: the light made the fence difficult to read. Dapples fell through the canopy of leaves, dancing in front of the fence, creating a slightly blurred effect, while the view through to the other side was much darker. Deciding it would be safe to approach this fence more slowly, as the ground on the take-off side was higher than the landing, Amber allowed Honey to trot, giving her more time to see and assess the fence. The pony gave no indication of being dismayed by the new obstacle, and when Amber put her leg on and gave an encouraging 'hup.' Honey obliged.

"Good lass!" Honey earned another grateful pat as Amber steered her into the woods and down the steps. *It's good that the steps are downhill*, Amber thought as she leaned back and let Honey hop down the staircase. *It's much less tiring for her than having to jump up them.*

They were soon over the two logs, up through the double of rails, over the monkey puzzle and on and off the Irish bank.

"Woah." Amber gave Honey the signal to slow to a walk, something Honey had never been asked to do on a cross-country course, as they approached the gate that had been set up in front of the water jump.

Pleased to have another chance to slow down and recover, Honey was a pro at helping Amber to negotiate the opening and closing of the gate. They were through in a matter of seconds.

"Come on girl, we're nearly home!" Amber steered Honey on towards the murky water jump which she'd recently had the dubious pleasure of taking a dip in when Molly tried to jump the whole thing. Despite the fact that she'd emerged from it looking like a swamp monster, the contents still looked as slimy as ever. Honey didn't turn her nose up at it though; she'd crossed this water jump before and it held no fear for her. The mud slurped at Honey's feathery fetlocks as she trotted through and, in no time, they were heading up the hill and over the penultimate fence: the railway sleepers.

They were clear and now all that was left was the dreaded final fence: the humongous wall. Even as Amber approached, she didn't know what she was going to do. The ninety centimetre wall looked truly enormous. Amber would have loved to complete the course with no jumping penalties and Honey had benefitted from her little rest at the gate, but she'd just cantered up a steep hill. Did she have enough left to take on the huge final fence?

Sensing her rider's indecision, Honey slowed to a trot, unsure what to do.

Taking Honey's unrequested transition into trot for weariness, Amber made her decision. She clicked her tongue to get Honey back into canter and pointed her at the lower, eighty centimetre wall; the alternative for her class. Honey picked up her feet and made a huge effort to clear the wide, solid obstacle. Amber patted her wildly all the way from the final fence until they crossed the finish. Part of her was disappointed to have picked up penalties for jumping the alternative, but the elation of completing the course clear made up for it. She couldn't control what happened to Emily or JoJo on the course, but she had done her part for the team. Honey had been fantastic around the biggest course she'd ever taken on. Amber couldn't have been happier.

As if to join in with the celebrations, Amber's stomach roared like a grizzly bear.

"Right, you wonderful pony. Let's get you sorted because I need to eat before I do the running. I could eat a horse!" Honey's ears flicked back as Amber spoke. "Oh sorry!"

She slid from Honey's back and was enveloped in a sauna-like quantity of steam. Barely able to hold herself upright, she led her brave little mare back to the trailer. There was still one phase left to go.

– Nine –

All Over

From being so weak she could hardly move, Amber now worried she wouldn't be able to run as she'd be so weighed down by everything she'd eaten after the cross-country.

When she'd arrived back at her trailer with Honey, she'd felt faint and her parents had found her propped up against the trailer's wheel arch, trying and failing to take Honey's bridle off. Her father had quickly taken over looking after the pony while Amber had been pushed to the ground by her mother. Mrs Anderson took off her daughter's riding hat, body protector and boots in a matter of seconds. She then pushed a water bottle into her hand and set the cooler containing all of her uneaten lunch, on the grass.

Amber was ravenous. All nerves were forgotten since the riding phase was over, but she was running on empty. The combination of anxiety and hunger had drained her. She ate as if the food was likely to magically disappear any second: sandwiches, crisps, mini sausages… she was just reaching for the chocolate when her mother stopped her.

"Better leave something for when you've finished," she said, returning the chocolate to the cooler and replacing the lid while Amber complained. "Your run is in less than an hour. If you eat any more, you'll give yourself stomach cramps. Just sit there, rest and digest. And take small sips of water."

Amber flopped back on the grass and closed her eyes, enjoying the sun on her face. Her body was exhausted; she could lie there and sleep forever. She had no idea how she was going to complete the run. But right now, she didn't care. She wasn't going to be the discount score and she had the best pony in the world. Her decision to bring Honey as her mount had been validated as there couldn't have been a pony all day who'd tried harder or been more cooperative with the slip rail and gate. Amber smiled to herself. She didn't care about the time faults she knew Honey would have picked up, as she suspected there would be a lot of riders here today with more than time penalties to worry about.

Eventually, Amber had to pick herself up off the grass and get ready for the final phase. Each competitor had been given a time to start their run as they were being set off individually, at intervals, to complete their personal race around the marked out running track. Amber wasn't looking forward to it. As well as being completely worn out, the running track was around the perimeter of the field used at the recent One Day Event for the dressage and show jumping. The field wasn't flat, which meant there were slopes to run up and down. To make matters even worse, the jumps and dressage boards had been put away as the field was being used to produce hay. It was already ankle-deep in thick, lush grass.

The majority of the field had been roped off to protect the grass, leaving just a narrow strip next to the hedgerow for the runners to stick to. Amber could see that the grass at the edge had already been trampled by the earlier runners, but this just made the track look lumpy and she knew it would hamper any attempts at smooth running. It was nothing like the flat, even surface of the cycle track that she'd been used to during training.

When she arrived at the start, she could see that five runners were already struggling on the track, poor Emily being one of them. Amber had no idea how far through her run she was, as they had to do three and three-quarter laps of the field to complete the 1,500 metres that was their set distance. Mr Pryde was standing near the finish yelling at her to keep going. At that point, Emily was running downhill but it wasn't helping to increase her speed. She looked as if she was about to stop moving.

As she watched, Emily passed through the finish cones and collapsed into the grass. Amber hoped it was because she had finished the distance and not because she just couldn't go any further. Amber had no idea what the penalty was for failing to complete the full distance of the run.

"Are you Amber from Blakefield branch?" a man with a stopwatch asked her.

"Yes, she is," Mr Anderson answered for her. Amber was busy watching Mr Pryde help Emily to sit up in the grass where she had landed. Emily looked like she wanted to shrug him off, but didn't have the energy to do so. She rolled a shoulder to remove her father's hand, but stayed where she was as another runner crossed the finish and almost fell over her.

"One minute until you start, okay?"

Amber turned her attention away from Emily and finished off her warm-up stretches. She'd recovered some of her strength after the feast she'd guzzled but still felt flat. She knew this wasn't going to be a good run. She always relied on people being in front of her to catch and overtake, but as everyone was running at timed intervals, that wouldn't be possible.

Stopwatch Man signalled that it was time for her to start so she set off, her parents cheering her on as she began the slog up the slope from the start. By the time she reached the top of the slope, she was already tired. The incline and the lumpy long grass made running uncomfortable.

But you've got a flat bit now, then a downhill and another flat bit before you have to go uphill again, she told herself, *so get your breath back and run as fast as you can on the downhill, as it won't take as much out of you.*

She soon became aware that Mr Pryde had noticed her amongst the other runners as she could hear him shouting her name and encouraging her to pick up her speed. *Oh, bog off!* she growled inwardly. *I'm doing the best I can.*

She opened up as she ran down the slope and along the flat stretch, through the finish cones for the first time, but she was soon back at the start and faced with the uphill section again. She groaned.

"Go on, Amber, accelerate up the hill! Pump it, use your arms. Faster!"

Amber said something unrepeatable in her head as she tried to block out Mr Pryde's constant 'encouragement'. It was annoying, but it probably did spur her on, just so that she could finish to shut him up.

As she began her final lap, the last effort up the hill was truly gruelling. Her legs wobbled and Amber considered dropping to a walk until she reached the flat part again.

"Go… on… keep… going… " She was overtaken by one of the older, intermediate boys, who struggled past her, breathlessly encouraging her, even though she didn't know him at all. *Poor thing*, she thought. *They have to run even further than we do*. Now that he was in front of her, Amber had someone to chase, and catching up to him became her focus. She didn't manage it, but by the time she ran through the finish cones for the final time, she was sprinting as fast as she could.

She didn't collapse in the grass like Emily had, although she definitely felt like it, but had to stand, bent over, clutching her knees for several minutes, fighting to breathe. She felt a hand on her back and saw Emily's patterned leggings and blue trainers through her blurry vision.

"Well done. That was a fantastic run," her teammate told her. "Your finish was amazing. You were flying! I was practically crawling when I finished."

Amber straightened up and looked into Emily's red, sweaty face.

"We did it!" she gasped. "It's all over."

"Yep," Emily laughed. "It's all over. No more blinking running for us. Now let's go and drink something fizzy and eat loads of chocolate. I think we've earned it today."

"Sounds good to me. Lead the way to the chocolate!"

- Jen -

There's no 1 in Team

Before the girls managed to embark on Operation Chocolate, Mr Pryde was shouting again. For JoJo. Although he'd only briefly seen JoJo at stable rallies and she'd never attended any of his training sessions, she was still part of their team, and so enjoyed the same level of encouragement from him as the other girls. Amber and Emily joined in with cheering on their final member, but it didn't appear that JoJo needed it. She ran like a gazelle, smooth and sure-footed over the undulations of the track. By the time JoJo swept through the finish cones for the final time, she was slightly pink and out of breath, but showed no signs of the exhaustion felt by Amber and Emily at the end of their run.

"Wow, that was fantastic," Amber praised. "You made that look a lot easier than it felt!"

JoJo nodded her acceptance, still catching her breath.

"Right, come on then," Emily linked both girls through the arms. "It's all done and there's nothing we can do now but wait for the results, so let's go and find Chelsea and pool our chocolate. It's time for a choc-fest!"

Chelsea was found sitting in the back of her dad's car, listening to music on her phone. She had to be coaxed out by a determined Emily, who refused to let her sit by herself.

"Come on, Chelsea. We're a team! Come and sit with us."

Chelsea looked uncomfortable at the mention of the team.

"You're a team, you three. My score will be dropped." She looked down, unable to meet anyone's eye.

"Nuh huh," Emily disagreed. "You've been brilliant in training and today was just bad luck. It could've happened to any of us. As my dad always says, 'there's no I in team.' Now get yourself out here. Bring any goodies you've got and come and sit with us!"

Amber understood Chelsea's despondency. She'd feared being the discard score, so she could imagine how disappointed Chelsea felt and how she'd believe she'd let the team down. And although Amber was pleased with her own performance, there was a strange sense of anti-climax now that the event was over. All the effort of training and the months of worrying about the riding phase were amplified by the fact it was for a team competition, but today, Amber had to admit, they hadn't felt like much of a team. Being spaced out as they were, they'd hardly had a chance to see or support each other and it had felt like she'd competed solely as an individual. She didn't even know how Emily and JoJo had got on with their cross-country round.

The four girls sat together in the grass, stretching out their tired legs, while they scoffed chocolate (Emily had brought a magnificent supply) and discussed the day, including Honey's unexpected appearance as Amber's mount. She was surprised that no-one said much about it, after all the worrying she'd done over what they'd think of her for not riding Molly. Relieved, Amber learned that, despite Pink's unenthusiastic start to the cross-country course, she had managed to get round clear, as had JoJo with Merry.

"That's great! We've got two clears then, probably with no time faults – so full marks for you two," Amber said. "I'll no doubt have some time faults and fifteen penalties for the alternative I took, but it should still be a decent score."

"It's seventy penalties for jumping an alternative," JoJo informed her.

Amber looked sharply at JoJo to see if she was winding her up, but the girl did not look like she was joking. Her blood turned to ice. "Seventy? What? It can't be. It was only fifteen penalties at the One Day Event."

"The scoring is different for Tetrathlons. It's seventy for an alternative but it's also sixty penalties for the first refusal, rather than the twenty it usually is. Then it jumps up to one hundred penalties for the second refusal," JoJo explained. She'd clearly done her research. "So, if we've gone clear with no faults," she indicated Emily, "we'll have scored the full 1,400 points available for the riding phase. But if you've only got seventy penalties and a few time faults, Amber, you'll easily have a high score too."

Amber took that in, trying not to feel too disappointed.

"My dad said there was carnage on the cross-country," Chelsea supplied. "He wasn't very happy with Skye getting eliminated, so he stayed out on the course to watch some more. The ditch caught a few out as usual: quite a few riders had problems there and had to take the alternative. Same with the water. The keyhole fence got a couple besides me and one or two riders didn't get past the first fence. And apparently, there was one rider whose pony wouldn't stop for the gate and jumped it! So, you three did brilliantly."

"Yeah, three ponies round with good scores in the riding phase will help to make up for my other phases," said Emily, plucking grass out of the ground.

The girls spent some time reassuring each other that everyone had played their part until they heard an announcement over the tannoy asking for competitors to assemble near the secretary's tent, which was actually a caravan, as the results were in. The girls dragged themselves off the grass and traipsed the short distance to where Brantfort Pony Club's DC, Mrs Winnaker, was bouncing with excitement to reveal the results of her newly reinstated Tetrathlon event.

Results started with the minimus classes. Amber tuned out of this slightly until she heard that JoJo's brother Matthew had come second in the team event and third individually. After the presentation of rosettes, it was time to move on to the junior section. The boys were presented first, drawing out the tension for the girls even longer.

"And now we move on to the junior girls' section," announced Mrs Winnaker. "We'll start with the team placings first. In fourth place, we have Copton Hunt. In third were West Hall Farmers. And now, we have a very close result between the first and second-placed teams," she added with a twinkle, enjoying the suspense she was building. "In second place, is our own Brantfort team, which means the winners are the Blakefield team!"

The four girls squealed and grabbed each other, hugging fiercely while their parents clapped and cheered.

"We did it!" squeaked Emily, unable to believe the news.

Amber didn't reply. She was too busy enjoying the look on her parents' faces. It was even better than in her daydream. She'd never seen them look so happy. They were as excited as the girls. Her mother, who didn't do public displays of affection, had grabbed Mr Pryde by the arms and was jumping up and down in front of him. He looked both pleased and bewildered at the same time. Her own father was ignoring them as he was looking at her. It was a look that said everything she wanted to hear.

After the presentation of the team rosettes, plus a mini shield each for Chelsea, Emily, Amber and JoJo, came the individual placings. Emily was shocked and delighted to have come fourth individually, and Amber was even more so to have been placed third. But no-one was surprised to see JoJo crowned the individual winner of the junior girls. She'd got full marks for the riding and led every other phase too. Her score was so far above anyone else's, she completely deserved the huge silver cup Mrs Winnaker presented her with. It was just like the one Amber had imagined.

"Wow. Congratulations!" The other girls stared in awe at JoJo's cup.

"Yeah, we'll have to do it again next year," Amber said, fondly stroking her lovely yellow rosette.

"Next year?" said JoJo, shaking her head. "Never mind next year. There's Area Tetrathlon in July. We can be a team again this year. Who's up for it?"

The other three girls looked at each other, communicating without words. All three of them had found the sport of Tetrathlon exhausting, frustrating and the biggest challenge they had ever experienced. They'd all faced self-doubt and disappointment in some way, yet they had won. There was no question about their reply.

"We're in!" they said in unison, grabbing each other to form a big, giggly group hug.

"We must be mad," Amber grinned, enjoying the feeling of inclusion. If JoJo had been mad at her during the competition, it looked like winning had restored their friendship.

"Absolutely bonkers," Emily agreed. "We're going to have to put up with my dad all over again. It really will be like preparing for the Olympics this time, I hope you realise."

"Bring it on," said Chelsea, pushing her shoulders back and raising her chin. "This is our chance to really be a team this time."

Her words echoed Amber's earlier thoughts. She was right. This time, they needed to work together more. Three out of the four of them had worries and insecurities about their performance in different phases of the competition, but they all had their strengths too. *If we support each other more, could we win at Area level?* Amber mused. *It's definitely worth a try*, she resolved.

– Eleven –

Unfriended

Their entry for the Area Tetrathlon was submitted by Mrs Best, their Pony Club DC, and accepted. The girls continued with their training, but now with JoJo joining in. She didn't really need to train, but they all agreed it would help them to feel more like a team if they spent more time together.

Sometimes they still ran on the cycle track behind the Prydes' house, but now the Prydes and Chelsea also travelled to the forestry to train on the tracks with JoJo and Amber. It was much harder running on the rough, hilly tracks of the forestry, but the recent branch competition had shown them that they couldn't expect a flat, smooth running route and they needed to be prepared for unhelpful terrain.

Amber was delighted that they were all now training together as it made them feel much more connected to each other. She was also happier about the idea of taking on another Tetrathlon following her better-than-expected performance in the recent branch competition. Emily, also, was so buoyed by her pony's clear round on a difficult course that she was throwing herself into the running and swimming. Even Chelsea had cheered up, recognising that she was strong in all the phases, except the shooting, and that her pony just needed more practice at cross-country having being used exclusively for show jumping until recently.

She'd been taking Skye to cross-country courses far and wide and reported that she was becoming much bolder and more reliable with the fences she'd previously had trouble with: ditches and jumps sited in shady positions. Mr Pryde helped her to practise her shooting whenever the running was taking place from his house and she was making good progress with her scores.

Three of the four girls seemed content, but strangely, the one who should have been the happiest and most relaxed didn't seem to be so. JoJo. Amber had noticed that JoJo seemed 'off' a while ago but she'd assumed it had been because she disapproved of Amber's decision to ride Honey instead of Molly in the Tetrathlon. But since Honey had done so well and effectively jumped clear round the troublesome course, Amber had thought that JoJo's mood would improve and she'd be forgiven. That was the impression she'd got after their win when JoJo was in high spirits. But JoJo remained taciturn whenever Amber saw her in training sessions. Hurt and confused with her friend's behaviour, Amber needed to know what was going on. She figured that if JoJo had 'unfriended' her, she deserved to know.

Warily, she texted JoJo to invite her for a ride out and was almost surprised when she agreed to come. Amber took Molly on the ride to be certain that she would keep up with Merry so that she could speak to her friend. She was relieved when JoJo rode out of her yard without her brother Matthew tagging along. They'd be alone.

The ride from JoJo's house to the forestry was almost silent, just punctuated with a few words of stilted small talk. When they reached the gate and found it closed, Amber knew that she should volunteer to get off and open it, as JoJo always had to. But she was still too frightened of what Molly might do when she tried to remount to offer. She stayed silent and, as usual, JoJo took care of the gate.

Once they were through it and on their way, Amber took a deep breath and started to speak, hoping that the right words would find their way out of her mouth.

"I was… er… a bit surprised you agreed to come today," she began, watching JoJo out of the corner of her eye to gauge her reaction.

"Oh? Why?" JoJo continued looking straight ahead, through Merry's milky pricked ears.

"Erm… well… you haven't seemed very… friendly recently. I thought you'd fallen out with me?" Amber inflected her voice at the end to suggest she'd like to know whether or not that was the case.

JoJo didn't reply immediately. There was just the sound of the ponies' hooves on the track and bird song in the trees as JoJo leaned forward to flick some of Merry's mane on to the other side of her neck with the rest. When she eventually spoke, her voice sounded husky and almost tearful.

"No, I haven't fallen out with you."

"Oh… it's just… since I told you I was riding Honey in the Tetrathlon, you seemed to go funny with me. I thought you were mad."

"What? Is that what you thought? Sorry. I was just having a bad day. But it was nothing to do with you."

"It wasn't just that day. It was all of the Tetrathlon day too, and since, in training…?" Amber pressed, relieved to hear that she hadn't been dumped. "You don't seem… yourself."

JoJo let out a sigh and slumped in the saddle. It was as if the breath she'd been holding had been keeping her upright. "It's… it's to do with friends at school. You know Nina?"

Amber nodded. Nina was JoJo's best friend at school. She wasn't into horses, but they'd been friends since infant school and had gone up to secondary school together the previous September. Amber had met her a few times at JoJo's sleepovers. She was slim, sporty and pretty, like JoJo. Although she hadn't said anything unpleasant to Amber, she hadn't felt comfortable in Nina's presence. Amber got the feeling she had a bit of a spiteful streak and felt sure she'd be making snide comments to JoJo about Amber's prominent teeth and frizzy hair the moment she wasn't in the room.

"Yeah," Amber replied, waiting for what was to come.

"Well, after Easter, a new girl started in our year and she was put in our form. Nina and I were asked to look after her, you know, make sure she knew where to go for lessons and lunch and stuff like that." She looked over at Amber, who nodded to show that she was listening. "But it ended up being more than just looking after her while she found her feet. She hung around with us all the time. I didn't mind. She was funny… a good laugh. And Nina liked her too. But… they started being a bit nasty to some of the… you know, quiet, shy kids. Nothing really awful, just saying mean things to them and laughing when they got upset. I didn't like it, but didn't know how to stop them."

They reached a part of the track where they usually had a trot. The two ponies started trotting without being asked, used to their routine. The girls didn't stop them and continued chatting side by side as the ponies trotted smartly along the long, flat track.

"Didn't you say anything to them? Tell them to stop?" Amber queried.

"No. I got the feeling that if I said anything, they'd start doing it to me. So… I didn't join in, but I didn't say anything either."

Amber considered asking if she could have told a teacher, but knew not to. Nobody wanted to risk being seen as a 'grass,' which was why bullying still went on.

"Not long before the Tetrathlon," JoJo continued, "Ellie invited me and Nina to a sleepover."

"Ellie's the new girl?"

"Yeah. So, when I got there, Nina was already there. After tea, we went up to Ellie's bedroom. She had all these posters of singers and bands on her walls. She wants to be a singer apparently. She suggested we sing along to some songs on YouTube, you know – the karaoke ones, and film each other. We did a few together then she said we'd do solos. It was good. But when I got home the next day and went on my phone, I saw they'd put the videos of me on Instagram with some not very nice comments. It turns out I'm not a brilliant singer – the videos sounded awful. At school the next week, everyone was calling me Karaoke Queen and Lady Blah Blah. I asked Nina why she'd done it and she said it was just a joke. But I could see her laughing when people were saying stuff to me… so… I shouted at her. I told her she was a… cow." JoJo whispered the last word, as if she was afraid of being overheard. The girls pulled the ponies back to a walk and Amber laughed out loud.

"Ha ha! What did Nina think of that?"

"She looked pretty shocked, to be honest. She didn't say anything but Ellie had plenty to say. Nina is with Ellie all the time now and I've lost my best friend. I've got other people to hang around with, but… so, anyway. If I've seemed a bit weird recently, that's why. Sorry. The Tetrathlon became something to focus on to stop me thinking about those two."

"No worries," Amber replied, relieved it was nothing to do with her and secretly pleased to hear there was something JoJo wasn't brilliant at. The imperfection made her more real. "Why didn't you tell me about it sooner, instead of bottling it up and keeping it to yourself?"

JoJo shrugged but didn't offer an answer. Amber guessed the words that hid, unspoken behind the shrug. JoJo didn't want to confide in her in case Amber's opinion of her was tarnished. In case she saw that JoJo maybe wasn't as perfect as Amber perceived. She didn't realise that showing some vulnerability actually had the opposite effect and made Amber like her more

"Sounds like you're better off without those two, anyway. You've got me and Emily and Chelsea. You can just concentrate on us and on trying to be Area Tetrathlon Queen, never mind Karaoke Queen! We can have our own sleepover. No singing involved."

"Ha ha, yeah, you're right. Thanks."

Amber grinned broadly, pleased to have cheered her friend up. She noticed they'd arrived at the bottom of the forestry hill and the ponies were starting to rev up, hoping to be allowed to race up it.

"Fancy a rematch?" Amber asked mischievously.

"You're on!" JoJo replied, pushing Merry into a gallop.

"You cheat!" Amber called to her, allowing Molly to chase after them. "Go on girl," Amber urged her pony. JoJo may have had a hard time recently, but Amber wasn't going to let her win.

- Twelve -

Hunting for Treasure

Amber rode every day: weekends and after school, stepping up Honey's workload to increase her fitness ready for the Tetrathlon. She continued attending Pony Club rallies with Molly and even started taking her to a few gymkhanas on Sundays for the show jumping classes. It was good to spend time with JoJo, Emily and Chelsea at rallies and shows, but despite Molly's excellent performance in all phases of the recent One Day Event, she seemed lacklustre when taken to a gymkhana to show jump.

Mrs Anderson had a theory that Molly was bored with years of show jumping and had enjoyed doing something different recently. And so, when she heard that Claire at Pine Tree Riding School had organised a Sunday treasure hunt for her clients, she asked if they could join in, on their own ponies. Claire thought this was a fantastic idea and asked Mrs Anderson to advertise it within the Pony Club, in case any other riders wanted to take part.

The day of the treasure hunt was red hot. Amber was excited as she was taking part with her Tetrathlon teammates, riding Pearl. Her parents were making up a team together and JoJo's mum was escorting Matthew and Emily's brother, Harry, who was bringing Fudge. Mrs Jones was going to ride Flash, who finally seemed ready to start working again after his accident. Amber wondered how Flash would take to being used as a babysitter as he'd always been a very highly strung and opinionated ride. Perhaps being unfit and weighted down by a heavier, adult rider would calm him a bit.

Emily and Chelsea were allowed to park their trailer and horsebox at Shaw Farm, as there would be limited space at Pine Tree. It meant they could all ride to the stables together, picking JoJo up on the way. Amber felt slightly out of place on Pearl compared to all the much bigger ponies, but she knew she'd have to take a turn today getting off to find the clues and she'd be perfectly safe doing so on Pearl. When she saw how Emily's pony,

Pink, had worked herself into a lather of sweat before she even reached the riding school from prancing sideways all the way down the farm track, she was pleased to be riding safe, quiet Pearlipops, even though she knew she'd end up being at the back of the group all the way round. Watching Pink trying to launch herself into one of her bolts, Amber knew that Emily was going to have a hard time and wouldn't be able to do any getting on and off.

When they arrived in the yard of the riding school, there was a melee of horses and riders that Claire and her head stable girl, Lisa, were trying to organise. When Claire spotted Amber, she called her over.

"Looks like you've got a good turnout for today," Amber said, taking in the commotion on the yard.

"Yeah, it's bedlam!" Claire looked harassed. "Do me a favour? I'm trying to set teams off at intervals with the clues in different orders so that everyone doesn't end up in the same place at the same time. You and Jo know the forestry well so can your team go and start now while I get this lot sorted?"

"Course," Amber agreed, taking a map, list of clues and answer sheet from Claire, all handily packed up in a plastic folder with a long string attached so that she could put it over her head and across her body.

"When you've got them all, or you've had enough, come back here. There'll be cold drinks and hot dogs ready once I've got all the riders away." Claire gave her a wave before hurrying back into the pandemonium of the yard, while Amber rode back to her teammates.

"We're first to start. Let's go!" And with that, they set off up the road towards the forestry, ready to start their hunt, Emily working hard to keep an excited Pink under control.

When they returned to the yard at Pine Tree, two hours later, it was strangely silent. All the horses and ponies were still out. The girls were able to hose the ponies to remove their sweat and cool them down, then they were allowed to turn them out into the small paddock beside the arena while they sat at the picnic table and enjoyed a cold drink and a tasty hotdog. Thanks to JoJo and Amber's extensive knowledge of the forestry tracks, they'd found all of the clues easily. Amber was feeling smug as she'd been the one who'd had to read all of the clues – some of which were pinned to trees, some on the ground, held down by stones – and record the answers, as Pearl had been the only pony who had stayed calm and steady enough for the task. The other three ponies had become wildly excited by all the charging about and the sounds of animated voices echoing around the valley when other teams located the clues.

They now had to use the first letter from every answer to the clues to form an anagram and rearrange the letters into a word that would be the final answer. The clue to help them solve the anagram was annoyingly vague: 'to do with horses'.

"That's a great help, I must say!" Chelsea chuckled.

"Ten letters, three of them A's. What can it be?" Emily mused.

"It's An – a –loo – e - an," said Amber, through a mouthful of hot sausage and onions dripping in ketchup.

"Er… what?" JoJo snorted, almost choking on her mouthful of food.

Amber swallowed and wiped her mouth. "Andalusian," she repeated. "Breed of horse."

"Oh yeah!" The others agreed, looking at the scrambled letters. "You're good at this, Amber." Chelsea nudged her in a way that was clearly meant to be friendly, but which nearly knocked Amber off her seat.

"We are the champions!" Emily sang as she wrote the word into the space for the final answer and rushed to hand it to Claire, just as other riders began to clip-clop back into the yard.

Amber beamed with happiness as she waved Emily and Chelsea off later and got into the car for the trip home. They felt like a proper team now. And more than that; they were friends. They'd laughed and chatted all the way round, as much as they could, while dealing with three prancing ponies. At one point, Emily had decided that they all needed a cool nickname, like JoJo.

"And since Chelsea's first and last names also begin with the same letter, she can be CC," she announced.

"Oh right, so what does that make you two then?" Chelsea asked. "EP and AA?"

"I'm not being AA. I'm neither a battery nor an alcoholic."

"Hmm, well, if you put the first part of both your names together, you get AmAn, but that doesn't mean anything." Chelsea mused.

"It could be AmAn-Da," Amber replied, more brightly. "Like Amanda McCarthy, the event rider."

"No, that's just, like, a normal name," Emily interjected. "You need something more unusual, more unique... I know! Ammo. You can be Ammo, as in short for ammunition. We are firing guns after all. And it rhymes with JoJo. Sort of."

"Ha, perfect for me, that, since I'm such a good shot," Amber joked, secretly quite pleased with her new nickname. "And what about you? Are you just going to be EP? Seems a bit dull for you. What else can you have? Something funny, like you?"

"I know," said JoJo, suddenly joining in. "Emily can be Teepee. And it rhymes with CC!"

"Oh great. Chelsea gets to be, like, a measure of power in an engine, Amber is bullets... and I'm a tent. I wish I'd never suggested it now. My name doesn't even begin with a T!"

At this, the girls laughed 'til their stomachs ached. It was one of the best days Amber could remember.

"Did you two have a good time?" she asked from the backseat. She hadn't had a chance to speak to her parents about their experience on the treasure hunt yet. Claire had asked them if they wouldn't mind chaperoning two of her adult customers who were competent novices and they'd been happy to help out. She noticed her parents exchange a brief look before her father, who was driving, looked in his driver's mirror and said to Amber's reflection. "Yeah, our two enjoyed themselves."

"Do you mean your two humans or our two ponies?" Amber joked.

"The humans. Definitely the humans." Mrs Anderson said before she could stop herself.

Amber noticed that her mother appeared tense. She was sitting stiffly in her seat, staring straight ahead. She hadn't had to ask Amber how her day had gone; she'd rambled on about every detail of their ride and how they'd won the treasure hunt, based on working out the final clue in the fastest time, when they rode back to the farm from Pine Tree. But now Amber realised that her mother had barely said a word since they'd got back to the farm.

"What's wrong?" she asked.

"Nothing," said Mrs Anderson.

Amber put both of her hands on the seat in front of her and pulled herself as far forward as her seatbelt would allow.

"What happened?"

"Oh, just Molly was a bit of a pain."

Amber went to say more but her mother silenced her.

"I'll tell you about it when we get home." Her tone of voice conveyed that Amber shouldn't ask any more about it. The rest of the journey home was silent.

Amber struggled to get to sleep that night. Why was it that as soon as something good happened, it was always followed by something bad? Everything had been going so well with the ponies and with the team and training, but now there was a problem. It was Molly. Again.

Over tea, Amber learned that Molly had been difficult on the treasure hunt. Firstly, she'd tried to bolt as Mrs Anderson was mounting her after she'd got off to read one of the ground level clues, and later on, she'd frozen and refused to move.

"What do you mean, she froze?" Amber asked, unable to understand what her mother meant.

"We'd just found one of the clues and the woman in our team had written it down. She, her husband and Dad rode away to find the next one and Molly wouldn't follow them. She just stood there trembling. I tried to coax her, then I got tougher. I even used the whip but she wouldn't budge. Eventually, Dad realised I wasn't there so he came back for me. He had to get hold of a rein and drag her to get her to move. She did go, but she was jittery for the rest of the time. I think it was all the noise of people charging around the forestry, whooping and hollering. She just couldn't cope with it."

Mrs Anderson stacked their plates and carried them over to the dishwasher.

"And as for trying to get on her... I can see what you mean now, Amber. It was a scary moment. No sooner had I put my foot in the stirrup and she was off! My foot came out and I nearly fell, but I had a hold of her so I unbalanced her and she stopped. Dad had to get off Honey and hold her for me to get back on. It's no wonder you didn't want to use her for the Tetrathlon when you had to do the slip rail. She's not safe."

She paused, preparing herself for what she was about to say next.

"Dad and I have been talking. We thought that some of the things that have happened with you and Molly were just down to inexperience and that, with lessons and time, you'd be able to manage her better. And you've done so well. You really have improved... but... seeing her behaviour today, I don't think she's the pony for you. There's something... not right about her. You've already had several scares with her and we think... well, we don't want you to have any more. We think it might be best to look for a new home for Molly, with a more experienced rider. We think it would be best for both of you."

Amber lay in bed with hot tears soaking her pillow. It wasn't so long ago that she'd come to the same conclusion about Molly and had been all set to tell her parents that she wanted to sell her. But then she'd made the decision not to give up, to give her a chance and to improve her riding. And then they'd discovered the problem with her saddle and got her a new one. Since then, things had been steadily improving. She wanted so much to be able to trust her pony, and she was getting there, apart from the mounting issue. But hearing about

Molly's strange behaviour today unsettled her. She didn't know what to do for the best.

- Thirteen -

Horse Whisperer

The next day they decided to let the ponies have a day off following the treasure hunt, but they still needed to go through to the farm after school to let Molly have an hour's turnout in the small paddock while they mucked her stable out and checked on the Fell ponies.

When they trundled past JoJo's house and rounded a bend on the pot-holed farm track, they came up behind Caroline, who was walking behind Lady with a lunge rope in each hand. Amber knew from the books and magazines she'd read about horse training that this was called long lining. There was nowhere for Caroline to steer the horse to let them pass, so they remained well back and crept slowly up the track and into the yard.

While Mrs Anderson led Molly out to the paddock to stretch her legs, Amber followed Caroline into the stable where she was unclipping the lunge lines and running the stirrups up on the battered old saddle Lady was wearing.

"How's she going? Have you ridden her yet?" Amber asked, patting the dark mare and smiling as her large ears flopped forward to enquire politely whether the girl had any treats for her.

"Not yet, but I will soon. I've just been doing groundwork to start with as I don't think she's had anything done since finishing racing. You can't just get on a thoroughbred straight off the track. They don't know how to be ridden in the way we ride." She pulled the worn old synthetic saddle from Lady's back and placed it on the stable door while she brushed the horse.

"They've only been used to the lightweight racing saddle with short stirrups for one thing. The weight of a normal saddle and a rider's legs hanging by their sides is unfamiliar. That's why I've been doing the long lining. I started in the paddock but she's been doing so well, I'm taking her down the track and back now. Pulling the stirrups down and having the lunge lines running through them helps get her used to the feel of things touching her sides. She's been fine so far, so tomorrow I'll try her with a leather saddle that's heavier than that old thing." She nodded towards the synthetic on the stable door. "And if that goes well for a couple of days, I'll start lying across the saddle and then progress to teaching her to be mounted. Racehorses don't ever have to stand still to be mounted as jockeys are usually just legged up while they're walking, so learning to stand at a mounting block can be a big deal for a lot of ex-racers."

"I'll have to watch what you do, see if it can help me with Molly's mounting problem," Amber said, carrying Caroline's brush box for her as they left the stable.

"Why? What problem has Molly got with being mounted?" Caroline enquired.

Amber reminded her about the accident at the forestry gate, nearly nine months ago and recounted her mother's tale of Molly's antics on the treasure hunt.

"I could help you if you like," Caroline suggested. "I've got an hour spare now before…" She left the sentence unfinished. Amber didn't notice; she was so pleased to have Caroline offer to help her with Molly.

Everything that Caroline said and did in relation to Molly so far had worked and Amber regarded her as a real-life horse whisperer.

"I'll go and get her!"

Amber ran to get Molly out of the paddock where her mother had just put her, excited to get started. Caroline wasn't giving up on Lady even though others had, and her calm optimism was infectious.

Caroline watched as Amber drew Molly alongside the mounting block in the farmyard and mounted her easily. Molly took a few steps away from the block as Amber swung her leg over the saddle but there was no sign of her bolting. Amber felt silly and rushed to say, "She's always fine here in the yard. She does it when she's out, away from home."

"Okay. Although… she didn't stand still for you just then, she walked away. Let's start with correcting that."

Caroline showed Amber how to make sure that Molly was standing square at the mounting block, so that she wouldn't be unbalanced when Amber got on, as this would mean she'd have to move to balance herself. "Also, you've got your reins quite tight as you're getting on. I know that's because you're worried about her moving off, but horses are actually 'into pressure' animals. She might be moving off to try and escape the pressure you're putting on her mouth. Try having a looser rein as you get on."

Amber wasn't sure about this idea. It seemed counter-intuitive, but she didn't want to argue. Caroline noticed her hesitation. "Don't worry. I'm right here. I can grab her if she goes to move."

Amber remembered Caroline's past advice about trusting her pony. Unfortunately, Amber didn't trust Molly, but she did trust Caroline, so she did as she asked. The first time she got on with a looser rein, Molly walked forward but Caroline quickly moved in front of her to block her. The same happened on the second attempt. But on the third attempt, Molly remained perfectly still.

"Well done," Caroline praised. "No, wait!" She stepped forward as Amber went to shorten her reins immediately. "You're giving her the signal to walk on straight away. Let her just stand for a while. Put your feet in and out of the stirrups, take time to notice whether you're comfortable and level in the saddle. Pick up your reins but then lengthen them again. Get her used to the fact she has to stand there until you put your leg on to tell her to move. She's just been doing what she thinks you want her to do as she's never been corrected. And I don't just mean you. This could be a habit formed from previous riders."

Amber had a few more attempts at getting on from the mounting block with looser reins, and to her delight, Molly remained stock still each time and didn't walk away until Amber told her to, even if she left the reins lying untouched on Molly's neck. "That's amazing." Amber laughed. "Clever girl." She patted the gleaming chestnut neck happily.

"Right, now let's go in the paddock and try her without the mounting block."

In the paddock, Caroline got a better idea of Molly's issue as she wouldn't stand still to be mounted from the ground at all. Calmly, Caroline told Amber not to mount by starting with her left shoulder next to the pony, facing her bottom.

"But that's how I've been taught to mount."

"I know, but look." Caroline took over and showed Amber what she meant by demonstrating. "When I stand facing her bottom and put my foot in the stirrup, I can't reach the far side of the saddle to pull myself up so I have to hop round like this before I can get my right hand over the saddle. I've wasted time, which is a bad thing for an impatient pony, plus, every hop I do can unbalance the pony and make it need to move to rebalance itself. Plus, if I'm not careful, I might stab her in the side with my toe as I'm turning myself round."

Amber watched, once again marvelling at how Caroline challenged the way other people did things by explaining it from the horse's point of view.

Caroline rearranged herself so that she was facing Molly's head. "If I stand like this, I'm close to her. I can get my foot in the stirrup, reach over to grip the saddle and push myself up and on much more quickly."

Caroline finished her demonstration by springing up on Molly so quickly the pony didn't have time to register what was happening. As soon as she felt the rider on her back, however, she stepped forward. Caroline gently pulled her back, but then dropped the reins, remaining on Molly for a few seconds while she stood still. Then she slipped off, giving the pony a pat.

"Your turn," she told Amber.

Encouraged by how easy Caroline made it look, Amber stepped forward eagerly. She got into position and tried to copy Caroline, but was dismayed when Molly walked away as soon as she went to pull herself up off the ground.

"Right, hang on." Caroline stepped forward and clipped a lead rope to Molly's bit. "It's a bit harder for you as you're not as tall as me, so reaching over the saddle is more difficult. It means you can't spring up as quickly. That's something you can work on though – being quicker in pushing up from the ground so you're not reliant on pulling from the saddle. If she's had back and saddle problems in the past, riders pulling on the saddle as they got on could have hurt her. That might be the root of this problem."

Once again, Caroline's words caused a lightbulb to turn on in Amber's brain. Of course! It was like Caroline could read the pony's mind.

"So now, try again. But hold onto this lead rope as you get on. If she moves at all, drop off and chase her on. Lunge her around you, basically. If she wants to move, let her move, until you see signs that she wants to stop: she'll turn her inside ear towards you, lower her head and

118

possibly lick her lips. When she does that, let her stop and try again. If she moves again, do the same thing. You need to get her to think that it's easier to stand still. If she doesn't, she'll have to work. Retraining is most effective if the horse makes its own choices, after being shown the options."

By the time they'd finished, Amber was mentally worn out. Molly hadn't been keen to be mounted from the ground and Amber needed to drive her on around her three times before she had managed a successful mount. She'd been so ecstatic when it had finally worked, she'd wanted to try again, but Caroline said that was enough for one day, and she should leave Molly to have some peace in the paddock for a little while.

"It's something to keep working on, little and often, to reform the habit. Then eventually, you can try it out on a hack. But not until she's completely reliable in here."

Amber held up her hand to high five Caroline. The young woman looked embarrassed but didn't leave Amber hanging.

"You're amazing!" Amber beamed as their hands connected. Caroline blushed and mumbled something before excusing herself and heading inside.

Amber removed Molly's tack and gave her a pat, letting her graze while she carried the saddle and bridle back to the tack room. Her mother was there, putting the mucking out equipment away, having finished cleaning Molly's stable.

"What were you up to with Caroline?" Mrs Anderson asked.

Amber filled her in on their impromptu session. "She's really good, Mum. I think she could cure Molly of her mounting problem. She's so clever, she even knows why Molly does it."

"Well, it's more an educated guess Love. No-one can actually know what ponies are thinking," Mrs Anderson countered, worried that Amber was getting her hopes up again.

"Go and pour cold water on it, why don't you?" Amber huffed, moodily.

"I just don't want you to think that Molly can be 'fixed' Love. She's not a machine. I think she's got some deep psychological issues that we aren't experienced enough to deal with."

"But Caroline is. And I know she's not a machine. That's why we have to give her every chance and not just sell her like a used car."

"Hmmm, we'll see. Anyway, let's not argue about it. We'll go and check the Fell ponies, then we'll bring Molly in and go home for tea. Come on."

Taking a hoof pick and a head collar each, they set off across the field where the Fell ponies were turned out to give them their daily check over. Upon reaching them, they immediately noticed that Honey's left eye was half-closed and weeping badly.

"Oh, Honeybun, what's happened here?" Mrs Anderson felt Honey's eyelid and detected some heat. "Have the flies been bothering you?"

Amber ran back to the tack room to get some cotton pads from the first aid kit. She soaked a few in water and Mrs Anderson used them to bathe Honey's eye.

"There you go, lass," she said stroking the pony's coarse forelock. "Hopefully that will help and it'll be back to normal tomorrow."

As the Andersons drove away, Amber thought about what they'd be having for tea and gave no more thought to Honey's eye. It would just be the flies bothering it and it would be fine tomorrow. There couldn't be any more bad luck heading their way.

– Fourteen –

Eye Eye

After dropping Amber off at school the next morning, Mrs Anderson drove straight on to the farm to check on Honey. She had the day off work and, while she was sure that the pony would be fine, since the Fell ponies never ailed anything, it had worried her all night. Even if it was just flies causing Honey's eye to water, she might need a couple of days indoors in the coolness of the stable to give her a rest from them.

But as soon as she caught Honey in the field, she knew the problem was far worse than an irritation caused by flies. The eye was now filled with cloud, turning it a stormy grey, and weeping with pus. The sight of it raised the hairs on the back of Mrs Anderson's neck.

"Oh no, no, no," she whimpered as she pulled out her phone and called the vet right from where she stood in the field.

The vet on call was busy, and the girl on the phone couldn't say how long it would be before anyone could come out, but if she could bring the pony to the surgery, she could be seen straight away.

"Damn!" cursed Mrs Anderson. Her husband was at work in the car that had a tow bar for pulling the trailer and her little car didn't have one. It looked like she'd have to wait for the vet, but she didn't like the idea of Honey suffering for hours before anyone turned up.

She brought the Fell ponies in and put them in their shared stable, using some cotton pads soaked in water to wipe away the worst of the pus oozing from Honey's eye. Then she turned Molly out into the small paddock and whizzed round her stable, cleaning it out in record time. She was just putting all the equipment back into the tack room, when she heard clip-clopping in the yard and popped her head out to see Caroline returning with Lady from a long lining session. She hadn't passed her on the lane so she must have taken her further today.

Mrs Anderson waited until Caroline exited the stable with Lady's tack before she hurried out and called her name.

"Hi," Caroline greeted her, then detecting the anxiety in the woman's demeanour, "Is everything alright?"

"It's our Honey," Mrs Anderson said, before going on to explain the state of the pony's eye and her predicament regarding the vet.

"There's a tow bar on the back of the Land Rover," Caroline said. "I'll just put all this away and I'll check with Dad that he doesn't need it. If not, I'll run you to the vet right now."

In less than fifteen minutes, the Anderson's trailer was hitched to the Blakely's Land Rover, Honey was loaded inside, Pearl had been turned out in the paddock with Molly to stop her becomingg frantic when Honey was taken away from her, and they were off, bumping down the rough farm track on their way to the surgery.

As the receptionist had promised, a vet quickly came out to attend.

"She's got an ulcer in her eye and uveitis I'm afraid," he said after adding some dye with a dropper and shining a light into Honey's cloudy eye. "I know it looks bad, but it's quite common. It can be caused by something simple like a hair or a hay seed getting in and causing irritation."

"So, what do we do now?" Mrs Anderson asked, clutching Honey's lead rope tightly.

"Well, that's the worst part of it. The treatment isn't very pleasant I'm afraid. We're going to have to scrape the surface of the eye to find the precise location of the ulcer, then she's going to need eye drops four times a day. She should wear a meshed fly mask at all times to block light and stop any debris getting in too."

"Yes, that's fine. How long do you think she'll take to recover? My daughter is meant to be using her for a competition in less than two weeks."

The vet sucked his teeth. "It depends on how she responds to treatment really, but she's not going to be ready for a competition in two weeks. This is likely to take at least a month, if not two and, once the eye itself heals, we'll have to check her eyesight to make sure it hasn't been affected."

Mrs Anderson gasped. "What, you mean this might leave her blind?"

The vet shook his head. "In most cases, horses recover their sight perfectly. But there is a small chance it could reduce her vision. That's why we have to be careful with the treatment. We'll start right now." He disappeared inside to fetch the equipment he would need and a veterinary nurse to assist.

"What am I going to tell our Amber?" Mrs Anderson whispered urgently to Caroline, even though there was no-one else there to hear her. "She needs Honey for the Area Tetrathlon! She's worked so hard training for it and she can't use that maniac Molly. What are we going to do?"

Caroline shrank away from the older woman's intensity. If she was looking to Caroline to provide any answers to this situation, she had none.

"I... I don't know," she stammered, looking at Honey's hooves.

"When are we going to get a break with these ponies?" Mrs Anderson ranted on. "It's just one thing after another with them. We should have bought Amber a blinking tennis racket instead of a pony!"

Caroline kept her head down, making sure she didn't get caught in the fire of Mrs Anderson's eyes. At the same time, a tiny smile tweaked her lips and a giggle formed in her throat. But she didn't let it out. She didn't dare.

- Fifteen -

Keeping the Faith

At first, the bottom fell out of Amber's world when she was told that Honey would not be recovered in time for the Area Tetrathlon. Her first reaction was a selfish one, concerning herself and the team. But when she saw Honey and how she stood, dejected in the stable, clearly hating her new fly mask, all her worries turned to the pony's recovery. The competition lost its place at the top of her list of concerns in comparison to Honey's suffering, and the possibility that she could lose the sight in her sore eye.

***

"You're still going to swimming?" her mother asked her when she presented herself on Friday evening with her kit bag ready to go to the final training session before the competition.

"I'm still going because I'm still doing the Tetrathlon," Amber replied, ready to retaliate against the protest she knew was coming.

"What do you mean you're still doing it? You haven't got a pony to ride."

"Yes, I have. I've got Molly and I'm doing it on her. Now get your keys and let's go."

Stunned, Mrs Anderson wordlessly lifted the sleeping cat who was curled in her lap and put him on the floor.

"Er... so..." she started cautiously in the car on the drive to the pool. "What's this about you riding Molly in the Tetrathlon? I thought you were dead set against it?"

"I was," Amber replied, "but Caroline is really helping me with the mounting thing and Molly is great at standing still for me in the paddock now. I've still got a week to practise for the gate using the one into the small paddock. It doesn't have a catch, just a rope over the stoop. Plus..." she added, "I thought you only got fifteen penalties for jumping an alternative on the cross-country but now I know it's actually seventy. Molly won't need to jump any alternatives, and if I do need help to get back on at the slip rail, that's only sixty penalties, so I'm definitely better off on Molly… and it's unlikely she'll get any time faults either. There's nothing to lose."

"Right," was all Mrs Anderson could say.

Amber was trying hard to convince herself that she believed what she'd told her mother. On paper, it made sense. She was likely to incur fewer penalties on Molly, even if she needed help to remount, and it was true that the pony would now stand perfectly still for Amber to mount her from the ground in the paddock. She'd even practised doing it with her stirrups shortened to cross-country length and she was much quicker at springing up now. But… she had yet to try doing it away from home. That was her challenge for tomorrow afternoon, after the final running session. She'd made some weird nonsensical pact with herself, and any god that might exist, that if she could stop stressing about Molly and just get on with the Tetrathlon with a positive outlook, rather than always focusing on how she might mess up, then Honey's eye would recover and she wouldn't lose her sight. She knew deep down that it made no sense, but she resolved to stick to it.

What did it matter, really, the result of a competition? She had to stop punishing herself for not being perfect and appreciate what she had. The situation put things into perspective and reminded Amber of what mattered in life. Honey had already showed her once before that winning wasn't everything, and she was delivering the same lesson again.

The next day she rode Molly to the forestry gate to practise mounting in the open, away from home. Although her heart felt like it was being juggled, and the voice in her head kept screeching furious warnings about her imminent demise, she ignored both of them.

Caroline and Mrs Anderson were already there to meet her, having bumped along the track in the Blakelys' Land Rover.

"Okay Amber, we're just here to help if you need us. But remember, you can do this. You've put the work in all week so just trust her and do the same as you've been doing," Caroline instructed as Amber slid from Molly's back and led her through the forestry gate. Caroline closed the gate behind them and clipped a lead rope on to Molly's bit, before handing it to Amber. "We needn't give her an escape route. Face her towards the closed gate when you remount and use it to block her from moving forward. In the competition, you can do the same with the slip rail. Once the top rail is back up, it can be used to block her. You still need to be ready for her spinning around in the opposite direction, but get on as quickly as you can, like you've been doing, so she hasn't got time to get impatient."

Amber took a deep breath and jiggled her shoulders to release the tension that was settling there. *I'm doing this for Honey*, she reminded herself. She could feel an uncomfortable trickle of sweat making its way down her spine. She noticed every millimetre of its journey and shivered suddenly, despite the warmth of the day.

"Right, come on you." She positioned Molly so that her head was facing the gate. Resisting the urge to gather her reins into a tight bunch, she left some slack in them, jammed her left foot quickly into the stirrup and launched herself straight up into the saddle. She prepared to grab the reins if Molly moved... but she didn't.

Amber laughed. "That's it! We did it!" she cried, unable to believe it had been so simple after all the months she'd spent worrying about it. "Easy peasy!"

Caroline smiled. "Well done. Now remember, don't gather your reins up and tell her to move just yet. Let her stand there on a long rein and wait for your signal."

Amber relaxed in the saddle and did as she was instructed. Molly actually sighed and rested a hind leg. Amber felt the pony's hip dip and she laughed again.

"Look how relaxed she is. She's going to have a nap!"

"I would never have believed this." Mrs Anderson turned to Caroline and put her hand on the young woman's arm. "Thank you. A week ago, I was ready to sell this pony. I'd nicknamed her Maniac Molly, but look at her now. You're a miracle worker!" Her eyes glimmered with tears of gratitude.

Caroline blushed and looked down at a clump of daisies growing in the grass verge. She noticed the delicate purple outlines of the petals as she spoke.

"I just showed Amber what to do, but she's done all the work. It wouldn't have happened if she hadn't kept at it and had faith that it would work. It was just a case of replacing an old habit with a new one," she told the daisies. "Now you all need to keep at it; anyone who rides her. Be consistent every time and Molly'll soon relearn what you want. The trick is to make it easy for her to do what you want and hard to do what you don't."

"Well, you make it sound so simple I don't know why we couldn't have thought of that ourselves." Mrs Anderson smiled as Caroline continued focusing on the daisies. "Right Love, you go and have yourself a nice ride and we'll see you back at the yard."

Amber slowly adjusted her weight in the saddle, sitting up straight and giving Molly a slight indication with her reins and legs to show that she wanted her to turn and move away from the gate. Molly did as asked calmly and they went on to have a lovely ride together.

"You're a good girl, aren't you?" Amber spoke to her pony in the silence of the forest. The pony's ears twitched to show that she was listening. "We've just taken a while to get on the same page. But I think we're there now, aren't we?"

Molly chose that moment to nod her head, making Amber laugh again. "You agree, girl?" She chuckled, patting Molly fondly. She knew the pony was probably just trying to dislodge an annoying fly, but she chose to see it as a sign. Everything was going to be okay.

– Sixteen –

All for One and One for All

The Area Tetrathlon took place over two days, which was a relief to Amber. *It should be far less tiring this way*, she hoped. But that was before she realised she'd have to get up at 4.30am to travel to the North East for the three phases taking place on the first day: the shoot, run and swim.

She sat in the back of Mr Jones' car, resting her face against the window, trying to stay awake. She'd slept over at JoJo's the previous evening so she could travel through with her the next day. Her parents, Mrs Jones and Matthew were following later with the ponies in the Jones' lorry. As far as she knew, Chelsea was getting a lift with the Prydes, and their ponies were also coming later in the day to stay in the overnight stabling, ready for the cross-country on day two.

The first phase, as with the branch competition, was the shooting. This time it was held in the gym of St Dunstan Grammar School. It was an impressive building, hundreds of years old and built from sandstone in the form of a manor house. It had probably been the home of Lord Somebody once upon a time. Now it was covered in ivy, giving it a rustic, homely feel, but the Latin motto, 'Gaudium et Scientia' carved into the lintel above the dark oak doors, gave Amber a shiver. It was probably saying something inspiring, but Amber found it intimidating. This school was nothing like her own, rather worn looking Wallam Academy.

When they arrived, the junior boys were shooting, so they were ushered to the back of the gym, where a tiered seating area gave them somewhere to sit while they waited for their turn. Amber and JoJo greeted Emily and Chelsea, who were already there, in whispers, aware that some of the groups of girls who were giggling loudly were being forcefully shushed by hard-eyed officials who glared at the offenders while pointing at the boys who were shooting. They were trying to keep the waiting groups quiet to allow the competitors to concentrate. This made some of the girls laugh even louder, drawing infuriated looks from the stewards.

"At least we'll all get to watch each other today," Chelsea said, quietly. "At the Brantfort Tetrathlon we hardly saw each other all day."

"Yeah, if you can see that far." Amber squinted at the boys in front of them. She couldn't even see the targets in the distance, never mind the bullet holes, to assess their scores. She searched her pockets for her glasses and had a heart-stopping moment when she thought she'd forgotten to bring them, until she remembered they were in her bag. Fishing them out, she placed them on her face and her vision cleared.

"Ah, that's better, but I still can't see their scores from here."

"Try these," Mr Jones said, handing her a heavy pair of binoculars.

Amber held them to her eyes and fiddled with the adjuster to bring them into focus. "Oh yes, I can see now!" she said, forgetting to whisper.

"SHHHHHHH!" She earned an angry stare from a steward.

As in the branch competition, the girls were called up one at a time for their shoot, keeping the same order they'd had before. While one shot, the other three crushed together taking turns to check out their performance through the binoculars. Chelsea was still the weakest shooter, despite the recent practice she'd had with Mr Pryde. Emily and Amber scored well, but JoJo leapt into a strong early position, getting at least eight of her shots in the bullseye.

Staying on the school site, the outdoor athletics track was being used for the running phase. Amber felt slightly disappointed for a second that their training on the steep, rough forestry tracks had not been necessary but soon recovered when she considered that this run would actually seem easy compared to what they'd done in training. Mr Pryde was obviously thinking the same thing.

"Look at this, girls. We couldn't have wished for better conditions. No struggling through long grass this time. You'll be able to fly!"

Amber thought this was a slight exaggeration, but compared to the running track they'd had at Brantfort's event, this was like heaven. 1,500 metres was further than

Amber was usually happy to run, but she was so much fitter now, thanks to all the training they'd done, she was almost looking forward to it.

Even better, because the running track had lanes, girls were being started in groups of four, to effectively race each other in heats. Everyone in the group was given a coloured bib to wear to distinguish them from the other group also on the track at the same time. Amber knew this style of running would suit her much better as she'd be able to keep her rivals in sight which would motivate her to build up her speed towards the end.

Chelsea ran first and easily beat the others in her group. As she rejoined the girls who were watching, waiting for their turn, she threw her red bib to Amber. Emily was on the track, running in yellow. She'd give her bib to JoJo when she finished. Amber was pleased that she got to run in red. She took it as a good sign as the Blakefield Pony Club colour was red and all the Blakefield team members were wearing red T-shirts to mark them as a team anyway. They'd been a surprise from Chelsea that morning. Her mum had had them made and Chelsea had presented each girl with their T-shirt after the shoot. The shirts had the Pony Club logo on the front, over the left breast, with the words 'Blakefield Junior Girls' Tetrathlon Team' embroidered around it. And on the back, the individual name of each girl was printed in large white letters, edged in gold across the shoulders.

"Oh, wow. These are awesome!" Amber had exclaimed, upon seeing her name on the back of her T-shirt.

"Yeah, this was so good of your mum," Emily agreed, hugging hers like a comfort blanket.

"We're definitely a proper team with these," JoJo added.

"There's more to come," Chelsea said, mysteriously. "But you'll have to wait and see. We wanted to do this as it'll be my only time on a team with you lot, at least for a couple of years, and it's been so good being on a team again." Chelsea's voice cracked slightly but she continued. "It's been a bit lonely, to be honest, since I gave up the gymnastics to concentrate on riding. I've been spending all my time training and competing Skye – on my own, as Imogen doesn't do it anymore – so, well it's been good to do this with… friends."

"What do you mean?" asked Amber, reaching out towards Chelsea but not quite touching her. "I'm sure

Brantfort will do their Tetrathlon again, and the Area competition runs every year too. We can do it again next year."

"Well, you three can. But I'll be fifteen in October, so this is my last year as a junior. If I do it next year, I'll have to move up into the intermediate age group. You could all be a team again though."

At that point, without noticing who started it, the girls hugged tightly and Emily declared, 'All for one and one for all.' JoJo's eyes sparkled with tears, which didn't go unnoticed.

"Oh God, I've made JoJo get all emosh!" Emily said, wiping tears from her own eyes. JoJo ducked her head and smiled. Amber had a good idea of why this display of friendship and team spirit had affected JoJo, but she kept it to herself.

***

As Emily's group completed their first lap of the track, Amber's group were called forward, ready to start.

Amber found herself in the inside lane. *Good*, she thought. *I can see everyone else from here.*

The other girls in her heat were placed in stages, ahead of her, in the outer lanes. The girl closest to her, in lane two, looked like her team's equivalent of JoJo. Apart from the fact her ponytail was dark, rather than blonde, she was tall, lean and athletic, like JoJo. She's the one to watch, Amber thought. The girl must have felt Amber's eyes on her as she turned around to look at her. Amber smiled at her, but it wasn't reciprocated. The girl regarded her with a look of disdain that reminded Amber of Elisha Templeton, an old adversary. Amber narrowed her eyes back at the girl and felt herself bristle with determination.

"On your marks," the starter called. The four girls in the heat got into position, ready to begin. "Go!"

Amber heard her name being cheered as she began and she noticed Mr Pryde on the sidelines, shouting encouragement to her before he turned his attention back to Emily. The Elisha-girl set off at a sprint and was soon flashing past the yellow-bibbed girl running in the same lane as her in the other heat. Amber didn't speed up. Maybe that girl was a proper athlete who could sprint 1,500 metres. Physically, it looked possible. But Amber knew she couldn't run like that and stuck to her tactic of getting into her rhythm and only building her speed towards the end.

As the red runners reached halfway through their penultimate lap, the yellow runners finished their race, leaving only the red-bibs on the track. The runner in the third lane had dropped behind in the previous lap, but the Elisha-girl and the girl in the outer lane were still ahead of Amber.

Right, Amber said to herself, *it's time*.

She pulled her shoulders back, opening her chest out, bringing her body into a more upright position. She lengthened her stride and, as her speed increased, she pumped her arms to create more power. Inch by inch, she gained on the lane four runner, drew level, and passed her. She could vaguely hear her name being screamed, but the blood rushing in her ears dulled the sound. The only thing she was interested in was the brown ponytail swinging ahead of her. Somehow, despite her body's desperation to slow down, Amber pushed harder and managed to lengthen her stride even more until she felt she was sprinting the fastest she'd ever gone. She didn't notice Mr Pryde hopping with excitement and screaming himself hoarse for her as she gained on her final competitor. All her focus was on Elisha-girl.

But it was too late. The girl had too much of a lead and finished just ahead of her as they surged over the finish line. Amber burned with disappointment as she gasped for breath, but at the same time, she knew that aiming to catch the girl had probably resulted in her running the best time she'd ever done. And when she caught the girl's shocked look as she realised how close Amber had been to catching up, it pleased her. Elisha-girl had obviously underestimated her.

Ha! Don't underestimate me, Amber aimed at the girl, mentally. *I'm ready for this, I'm in a brilliant team, I've got an amazing pony and I'm doing this for Honey*.

She remembered how weak and enervated she'd felt at the last Tetrathlon, only weeks ago. It seemed like years had passed. Like she was an older and stronger version of herself and that other Amber was long gone, replaced by someone strong and positive.

She liked it. She'd felt like this once before, when she silenced Elisha Templeton's criticism of Honey by getting a clear round in the pony's first ever attempt at cross-country. It hadn't lasted then; she'd lost her confidence again, and the self-doubt returned with a vengeance, but this time, she embraced it.

Old Amber can stay where she belongs, in the past, she thought. *This Amber is much better.*

With that, she went to rejoin her teammates and watch JoJo's run.

- Seventeen -

The Calm Before the Storm

After a long leisurely lunch in the school's courtyard, where there were picnic benches and seating arranged around the fruit trees and flower beds, it was time to head back inside for the swimming phase.

"What kind of school has a pool?" Emily asked Amber.

"One that's a bit posher than ours," Amber joked.

As the girls headed into the changing room, they bumped straight into Elisha-girl. She looked them all up and down with that supercilious air she had, lingering on Amber.

"What are you like? The exclamation mark on the end of your team?" she asked in a Geordie accent.

"Er, what?" Amber asked, uncertainly.

"Well, these three have all got a bit of shape to them, haven't they?" She nodded towards Amber's teammates. "And then there's you on the end, built like a stick with that massive mop of hair. You look like an upside-down exclamation mark!" She looked to her teammates for approval and they all giggled obediently.

Amber turned as red as her T-shirt. All recent thoughts about her new strong and positive self withered like an autumn leaf. Elisha-girl, already in her swimming costume, smirked, clearly pleased with the effect of her words.

Chelsea moved with the agility of a leopard and pounced on the girl, pinning her shoulders to the lockers behind her. Elisha-girl squealed, possibly out of surprise or possibly because a locker key was digging into her back.

"What did you say?" Chelsea snarled in the girl's face.

Her opponent was shocked, but she stared back at Chelsea, radiating hostility. Although her attitude was defiant, she kept her mouth shut.

"Say anything like that to one of my friends again and I'll knock your teeth out." Chelsea released her grip on the girl and she hurried away, glancing behind her as she headed towards the showers with her teammates. They weren't giggling now.

Shaking her head, Chelsea stalked over to the lockers on the other side of the room and yanked one open. She began taking off her trainers and socks, placing them in the locker. The other three girls stood and stared at her back. None of them moved or spoke. Feeling their eyes boring into her, she turned around and regarded them.

"What?"

"Chelsea… that was, like, a tad aggressive, don't you think?" JoJo said what Amber was thinking.

"Aw, she was just a little bully. She deserved it. These bully types need squashing before they get going. I've met enough of them through gymnastics – they're like boa constrictors. If you let them sense any weakness, they'll squeeze and squeeze until they've crushed the confidence right out of you."

She made her hands into claws and mimed squashing an imaginary foe.

"That's what she was trying to do to Amber because she ran so well: intimidate her to try and spoil her swim.

We don't need to worry about her now though. Bullies are always wimps."

"Wow," breathed Amber. "You're like our own Katniss, Chelsea! This girl is on fire!"

Chelsea chuckled and turned back to her locker, pulling her shorts off and cramming them in, on top of her trainers.

As the girls got changed, Amber developed her earlier train of thought. "If you were a fictional character, Emily, who'd you think you'd be?" Emily cocked her head and thought about it for a moment.

"Erm, maybe Jo March... from Little Women."

Amber looked at her expectantly, waiting for an explanation.

"Well, she's quite independent and creative like me, not very girly, but she's got good hair," Emily tossed her dark curls playfully. "What about you?"

"Oh, I'd say I'd be Hermione. I've got the hair and I've heard lads at school calling me a swot, so I'm a good match." Amber's long, thick golden hair had always been her best feature, but since she'd become a teenager, it had dulled to a mousy non-colour and turned coarse and frizzy. She fought it into a bun on top of her head and secured it with two bobbles to keep it out of the water.

"Yeah, but Hermione's got a feisty side to her, remember. She slapped Malfoy," Emily pointed out. "Not that I'm condoning violence." She aimed her comment towards Chelsea.

"Ha ha, yeah, says the girl who slapped Elisha Templeton," Amber reminded her. "You've got Jo Marsh's quick temper too!"

Emily shrugged. "Touché. But that was a one-off. Elisha pressed a red button that day. I've never done anything like that before; I'm normally super-chilled." She closed her eyes and touched her index fingers to her thumbs, imitating a meditation pose.

"Who'd you be JoJo?"

"Um, I dunno." JoJo didn't look at Amber as she kicked off her Skechers.

"I do," said Amber. You'd be Diana, Amazonian warrior, AKA Wonder Woman, sent here to lead us to victory!"

"Yeah right," JoJo replied modestly, but Amber could see she was smiling.

***

That night, the team set up camp at Farley Park Equestrian Centre, where the next day's riding phase would be held and where the ponies were being stabled. Once the four ponies were fed and bedded down, and the cross-country course had been walked, the three dads set up a barbeque for everyone. It was an enjoyable evening sitting outside in the balmy summer weather. There was plenty of food for everyone and the team delighted in filling in the adults, who'd only recently joined them, about the day's exploits, though they left out the small detail of Chelsea's altercation with the Elisha-girl at the pool.

All of the girls had secured personal bests in the swimming that day. Their team spirit was rocket fuel, giving every girl extra energy to push herself to her limit. Amber lived up to her new nickname, using Elisha-girl's poolside comments as ammunition against her when she tried again to derail her confidence. As they waited to be told to take their places for their heat to begin, Elisha-girl looked Amber up and down, tutting and muttering, "tragic," quietly, but so that Amber could hear her. Amber did nothing to retaliate until she hit the water and ploughed up and down the lengths like a pro swimmer. Success would be her revenge.

Even Mr Pryde had congratulated them all, acknowledging that no-one could have tried any harder. He'd given Emily a huge hug and told her she was a warrior. Emily had shrugged him off and told him that he was the most embarrassing dad ever, but Amber knew how pleased she was underneath the bravado.

After the swimming, the team had been driven to the equestrian centre where they hadn't had long to wait before the ponies started arriving. Mrs Jones and Amber's parents were first, bringing Molly and Merry in the Jones' lorry. They'd unloaded them and got Matthew to help with opening the bales of shavings in their stalls to stop him from sulking that he wasn't competing.

"Maybe next year," Mrs Jones consoled him. Matthew's problem was his pony, Sam. Although Sam was perfectly reliable at jumping a short course of small fences, he wasn't the pony to jump round a twenty fence, eighty centimetre cross-country course. He'd been great for Matthew while he was learning, but now he yearned for something with a bigger engine. Amber sympathised as she knew exactly how Matthew felt. It had been the

153

same for her with Pearl. But she'd been lucky enough to keep Pearl when Molly was bought for her. Would Sam be able to stay with the Jones' or would he have to go on to a new family and show another young learner rider the ropes? Amber's heart ached at the thought of the pony leaving his home.

Soon, Mrs Pryde pulled up and Pink was the next pony into her overnight stable. Matthew looked hopefully for Harry, Emily's brother, but he wasn't there.

"Oh, I'm sorry Matthew, Harry's staying with his grandparents tonight. I didn't know you'd be coming."

Matthew's face fell. With no-one to hang out with, he hid away in the lorry with his Gameboy until the barbeque began and lured him out.

The last to arrive was Mrs Connor, bringing Skye in their small, gold horsebox.

"Oh girls, the T-shirts look great," she said, pleased to see they were all wearing their new team tops. "I've got something else to show you. Come on."

Intrigued, the girls followed her back to her little lorry where she opened the tack locker and rummaged around, before dragging several plastic bags out and dropping them on the grass. The girls, except for Chelsea, who already knew what they contained, waited expectantly as the items within were revealed.

"Team saddlecloths!" Mrs Connor announced, holding up a bright-red saddle pad with 'Blakefield Pony Club' embroidered into one corner in white. "One for each of you," she said, passing one to them all. "You can't keep these I'm afraid. I'm going to donate them to the club after you've used them, for future teams, but you'll be the first to ever use them! And also… " She did some more rummaging in another bag. "Team colours too!" The girls were all handed a package which contained a red base layer with large white stars on the sleeves and a red hat silk, also with white stars on it. "I know you'll all have your own cross-country colours, but I thought it would be nice, for a team event, if you were all matching." Mrs Connor looked at the girls hopefully.

"Oh, wow, these are AH – MAYZ - ING!" Emily gushed, her eyes shining as she drank in the Ferrari red package in her arms. "Thanks, Mrs Connor!"

"Yeah, thanks. They're brilliant!" echoed Amber and JoJo.

"Knock 'em dead tomorrow girls." Mrs Connor was clearly relieved that the gift was well-received.

Eventually, the sausages and burgers ran out. The sky gradually darkened and the camping field quietened as people started disappearing into their lorries and tents to sleep. The Blakefield group tidied up their mess, gave the ponies a last check and started to do the same. The Jones' were sleeping in their lorry, Chelsea and her mum were in theirs and Amber was bedding down with Emily on blow-up camp beds in Emily's trailer. Their parents were heading off to a local B & B for the night.

"Are you nervous for tomorrow?" Emily asked Amber, once they were both in their beds, breathing in the lingering scents of hay and horse poo as they waited for sleep.

"Yeah. But not in the usual way," Amber pondered, struggling to find the words to explain herself. "It's... more like... excited nerves rather than scared nerves, if that makes sense. I think tomorrow is going to be okay."

"Me too," Emily murmured before yawning.

In no time, the girls were enveloped in a deep, happy sleep filled with dreams of flying over cross-country fences and being presented with gold medals.

Outside, the cross-country course awaited them, the fences crouching in the darkness while the ponies and people drowsed peacefully. It was the calm before the storm.

– Eighteen –

The Heat is On

On cross-country day, Amber and Emily were up and dressed by 6am, unable to bear the heat inside the metal trailer and their sleeping bags.

"Urgh, it's gonna be a scorcher!" Emily squinted up into the cloudless blue sky, shielding her eyes from the sun.

The yard was already alive with the sounds of clanking buckets and the swish of brushes sweeping the ground. The muggy night had made sleep difficult for everyone and drew them out early in search of a cool breeze. Unfortunately, the air outside was just as hot and still as it was inside.

Chelsea and JoJo emerged as Amber and Emily were preparing the morning feeds. Chelsea was full of energy and didn't seem to notice the stifling heat. JoJo, on the other hand, looked uncharacteristically sleepy.

"All right JoJo? Good night's sleep?" Amber asked as she put Molly's feed bucket inside her stable. The pony ate eagerly, standing on three legs as usual as she picked up her front left hoof and held it as if an invisible person was inspecting the sole of her foot. JoJo stretched and yawned noisily.

"No, I flipping well didn't. I had to sleep next to Matthew and I'm sure he was doing kung fu or something in his dreams. He's thumped and kicked me all night. I nearly pushed him out of bed at one point."

"Yeah, I know what you mean," Emily called from Pink's stable. "I had the same trouble with Amber talking in her sleep all night. Couldn't shut her up. I never got a wink of sleep either."

"No, I didn't!" Amber exclaimed. "Did I?"

Emily just smiled but didn't reply.

"Well, what did I say then?" Amber asked.

"Oh, I'm sure you'd rather I not say in front of everyone. I wouldn't want to embarrass you."

"You're joking, aren't you? I didn't talk in my sleep, did I? Emily? Em?"

Emily's smile widened and a giggle escaped her, but she didn't reply, enjoying winding Amber up.

"Has anyone seen my bridle?" Chelsea flustered a little later. She was the first of the team to ride and the girls were all together to help her get ready. "It's not in the tack locker! I asked Mum if she brought it and she said she did. And I can remember seeing it yesterday when I checked. But now it's gone!"

"Okay, okay. Calm down. It has to be somewhere. Let's have a look," suggested Emily. "You definitely haven't hung it up outside your stable or something?"

"No! I've looked everywhere. It's not here!"

The girls looked all over the stable areas where all the riders' ponies from the different teams were, but there was no sign of a bridle that matched Chelsea's description. They checked all over Chelsea's lorry and even looked in the Jones' lorry and Emily's trailer. But the bridle couldn't be found.

"What am I going to do?" Chelsea wailed. "I'm on in half an hour. I should be warming up by now and I'm not even tacked up!"

Emily took control of the situation. "Right, calm down. All of our ponies are about the same size. You can borrow one of our bridles. We're all on later so it'll be fine."

"But none of yours have the same bit I use for Skye! Molly and Merry are both in snaffles and what do you ride Pink in? A pelham?" Chelsea was shaking as she started to put Skye's boots on.

"Yeah," agreed Emily. "Why, what bit do you use?"

"A tranz universal."

"What's that for?" asked Amber, who had no idea about bits beyond snaffles.

"It just helps me to turn her when we're doing fast work as she can be heavy to steer. It gives me better control if I have to shorten her too. She tends to throw her head around otherwise."

JoJo had quietly saddled Skye, so besides her bridle, the pony was ready to go.

"Right, we'll bridle her for you while you get your body protector and number bib on. Which do you want? Pink's pelham or Molly's snaffle?" Emily steered Cheslea out of the stable.

"Oh, God. This is terrible. She hates a pelham so I can't use that but she'll be awful in just a snaffle too. I don't know what to do!"

Emily made an executive decision. "Well, if she hates the pelham, that will just upset her and tire her out quickly so we'll go with the snaffle. You're as strong as an ox so I'm sure you'll manage her. The course is long and it's hot, so hopefully she won't have the energy to be too argumentative. Right, hurry up."

She shooed Chelsea towards her lorry to get what she needed from her mum, who was busy chatting to the other parents and not being very helpful. "Amber, fetch your bridle," she commanded.

Chelsea made it to the collecting ring to warm-up and have her tack checked with only ten minutes to spare before her start time. All of the team members and parents were there to see her start and finish, but they wouldn't be able to watch the course as it crossed five different fields and there was nowhere to stand from where a large part of it could be seen. Instead, the supporters sat on a bank behind the collecting ring, guzzling water from the bottles Mr Pryde had produced from the boot of his car that morning. The water was unpleasantly warm, but it was so hot already, they would have drunk anything to quench their thirst.

They couldn't see much except the start and finish, but there was a commentator who was reporting on the riders' progress around the course on a loudspeaker. It gave the competition a much more professional feel to it than Amber had experienced before, and her stomach lurched at the thought of her turn, waiting for her later in the day.

Soon, they could see Chelsea being summoned over to the start. She looked amazing on her bright white pony, with the new red and white colours. In no time, she was into the start box and away. The supporters cheered as the commentator announced her, and the girls breathed a sigh of relief as they watched Skye jump over fence two and disappear into the woods that lay on the other side.

"Chelsea was worried about that fence," Amber explained to the adults, "as it goes from light into darkness. Fences like that have been Skye's Achilles' heel in the past."

"Yes," Mrs Connor agreed. "Chelsea has worked so hard with her; I hope she gets round today. I know she's worried about the trakehner fence near the end too. Even the alternative is an open ditch and ditches aren't Skye's favourite thing either."

They listened to the commentator as he reported on the riders currently on the course. Chelsea had got to the gate with no problems, and was through it quickly, but after that was a long downhill slope with a double of angled rails at the bottom. Chelsea jumped the first part but... oh no! She'd missed the second and had to come back for it.

"Like she said: steering problems," Amber whispered to her teammates.

"Yep, that's sixty penalties," JoJo whispered back.

After the problem at the rails, Chelsea's round continued smoothly. When they heard that she'd ridden straight over the dreaded trakhener fence, they all cheered. It was a real rider frightener: not only did it have the angled rail above a wide ditch, it was topped with a row of luminous green artificial brush. It was truly terrifying to behold and Amber knew, if there was any fence she was likely to wimp out at when her turn came, this was the one.

But Chelsea was over it, through the slip rail, straight through the double of corners and the next thing, they could see her splashing through the water jump and cantering on towards the final fence, parallel to the first: the flower box.

It was a shame about the sixty penalties but it was a huge, tough course. When Amber had walked it the previous day, she was relieved that she had Molly as her mount. She so hadn't wanted to use Molly for this competition but it was like Fate had intervened. The course was long, with twenty obstacles, plus it was hilly and the fences were either enormous, or technical, or both. There was no way Honey would have managed to get round it. And now, with this heat to deal with, the course was doubly difficult.

Chelsea slid off Skye once she was clear of the finish and loosened her girth. Her face was the same colour as her top and hat silk. The girls ran to her, full of congratulations. Emily took Skye's reins to lead her back to the stables while Amber pushed a bottle of water into Chelsea's hands. She drank the whole thing in one go.

"She… was… brilliant!" Chelsea gasped, still out of breath. "But… so… strong! Couldn't… steer… downhill… double… ran… right… past… it."

"Don't worry about it," said JoJo. "I'm sure that course will cause all kinds of trouble today and you're one of the first to ride it. You can just relax and watch everyone else now. I just wish we knew what had happened to your bridle."

With that, they approached the stable block. Rounding the corner, leading the pony, Emily was the first to see Skye's stable.

"What the… ?" she said, pulling Skye up.

"What is it? What's up?" Amber asked.

The other three girls caught up and stood beside Emily, looking at Skye's stable. Lying in front of it, in a crumpled heap on the ground, was the missing bridle.

- Nineteen -

Rock the Boat

"And our next starter is Emily Pryde, riding Sunset Friday for the Blakefield branch," the commentator announced as Emily left the start box on board Pink.

The Blakefield team members and supporters were back on the bank behind the collecting ring to listen as Emily's round began. Amber and JoJo had to keep shushing Chelsea as she ranted about her bridle. Ever since it had been found, dumped in front of her stable after her round was complete, she'd been convinced it was down to Elisha-girl.

"Who else could it have been?" she hissed again as she sat on the bank. "No-one else would have had reason except her. She'll have done it as some kind of revenge against me for what I did in the changing room. You can see she's that type; mean, jealous, spiteful." Chelsea ripped handfuls of grass out of the ground in front of her and shredded them. "After all the effort I've put in to prepare Skye for this, I've got a good mind to get her back. I could hide her hat, or her saddle or…"

"Chelsea, I'm sorry but you need to stop going on about it," Amber whispered harshly. She'd just heard the commentator say that Emily was over the brush with the open ditch in front of it at fence five and was now heading up the hill. "We've no proof that it was her and you still did really well. Let it go. You're not doing anything to retaliate so just leave it."

Chelsea stared at Amber for a moment before she went back to ripping grass. "It's okay for you, it didn't happen to you," she mumbled. "I could've gone clear. Would've gone clear if it wasn't for her. All that time I've put in…"

Amber chose to ignore Chelsea and focused her attention on the commentator. It was her turn to ride next, and she was starting to feel the usual nerves awakening inside her. In an attempt to numb them and prevent them from starting their usual all-out-party in her stomach, she was trying not to think about them, and distract herself in any way possible. Right now, that was by listening to Emily's round.

Emily had managed the double of angled rails where Chelsea had her problem, and was going well, approaching the dreaded trakhener. She was over it! There was a pause in Emily's progress report while the commentator introduced another new starter and by the time he came back to Emily, she was splashing through the water jump and heading to the final fence.

"It looks like she's gone clear!" Amber stood up and clapped her hands, delighted for her friend.

But just as Emily cantered through the finish, patting Pink furiously, her face beaming, there was an announcement from the commentator.

"I'm afraid to say that Blakefield branch member, Emily Pryde, has been eliminated for missing out fence number eighteen."

"What?" Emily's face fell. "I didn't miss anything out. Which fence is number eighteen?" she asked her teammates who were surrounding her as she slid to the ground.

"Eighteen is the upturned boat before the water," Chelsea reminded her.

"*What*? A boat in front of the water? There wasn't a boat in front of the water! It was the double of corners, then the water." Emily's eyes pleaded with the girls to confirm she was right. They looked at each other as they realised what had happened.

"No. After the corners, well over to the right, there's a boat. You have to swing round to it. The water jump is fence nineteen. We walked the course together. How could you not have seen it? Did you not pay attention to the numbers on the fences?" Chelsea's bad mood left no room for tact.

"But I was clear!" Emily sobbed. "I was clear." She buried her face in Pink's sweaty neck. Her shaking shoulders were the only sign of her anguish as she cried in silence. Amber and JoJo tried to console her, but soon Emily's parents were by her side. They fell back as Mr and Mrs Pryde escorted Emily back to the stables. Emily's mother had her arm around her daughter, but Mr Pryde was too irate to deliver any sympathy. "I'll put in a complaint!" They could hear him declaring as he walked away, leaving them behind.

"Oh, shut up, Phil," Mrs Pryde snapped at her husband.

170

"I'd better get Molly ready," Amber said. The fact that Emily had jumped clear around the course had inspired her and helped to tuck her nerves away slightly but now that Emily was eliminated, they were back, disco dancing with the music turned right up.

The pressure was on. Again. Emily's score would now need to be the discount and Chelsea had picked up an expensive sixty penalties. JoJo was bound to go clear, but they couldn't win with just one clear round. She needed to go clear too. And that meant no jumping any alternatives and no help remounting at the slip rail. Why couldn't Emily have jumped the boat? Or Chelsea have had her bridle? Just for the sake of those simple things, there was now a massive spanner in the works.

Amber felt the panic rising within her. She didn't do well under pressure. *I can't do this*, she thought.

YES YOU CAN, she told herself, forcefully. *Think positively. Picture yourself riding well on the course. Visualise what you want to happen and then make it happen. Don't clam up and don't put pressure on yourself. Lives aren't at stake here. Go out and enjoy yourself.*

Amber blinked rapidly, shocked at the talking to she'd just given herself.

"Are you okay?" JoJo asked her, as Amber had stopped walking and stood, as if in a trance.

"Er, yeah… just thinking. And I'm hot!" Amber shook her water bottle but only a few drops remained. "I need a drink," she declared, heading over to one of the food stalls. *That'll make me feel better*, she decided.

"Sorry, sold out of drinks," the vendor told her, sweating as he flipped burgers.

"What am I going to do? I'm gasping!" Amber moaned to JoJo and Chelsea.

"I'll find you a drink. You go and get ready," JoJo told her.

When Amber arrived at Molly's stable, she found her parents already there, saddling the pony for her. Molly was doing her customary gnashing as the girth was done up. The pony looked amazing with her white boots and bright red saddle pad bearing the club's logo. The colour suited her. She looked so professional, an image of her favourite event horse, Zero Fox, jumped into Amber's head. The idea that she was about to ride round a cross-country course on a pony who looked exactly like a famous five-star event horse had a strange, dream like quality to it.

"We've got Molly sorted," her mother said. "You go and get yourself ready. Don't rush. You've got plenty of time and it's too hot to be dashing around today."

The day did seem to be getting hotter. By the time Amber had changed into her full cross-country outfit, she was baking. JoJo had managed to source another bottle of water from somewhere. Amber didn't bother to ask as she gratefully took it and drank half of it in one go.

"Right, save the rest. You'll need some when you finish and there's a water shortage out there. Ration it or you'll be drinking from Molly's water bucket when you get back!"

JoJo took the bottle and slapped Amber on the hard shell of her body protector. "Go and get on. We'll be watching and willing you on. Good luck."

JoJo and Chelsea headed away together, back to their spot on the bank where they'd watch her warm up and listen to the commentary on her round. Amber appreciated that neither of them had said anything to put pressure on her. They could probably tell by looking at her that that was the last thing she needed right now.

Mrs Anderson tried to hold Molly as Amber mounted her before heading down to the collecting ring, but Amber stopped her. Although she was trembling with nerves, this was her last chance to practise. Molly could clearly tell that something exciting was happening. She lifted her head high and pricked her ears. Her face twitched as she picked up the sound of the loudspeaker in the distance.

Amber pushed out a deep breath and patted the pony's already slightly damp neck, forcing herself to relax. "Easy girl. Just stay nice and calm. We're going to go and have some fun but it's nothing to get worked up about."

She remembered Caroline telling her that Molly would pick up on her own anxiety and react to it. She needed to be quiet and assured, but quick. And so, forcing herself to leave some slack in the reins, she quickly stood next to Molly. Facing her head, she jammed her foot in the stirrup and leapt up into the saddle in one swift motion.

Clearly intoxicated with the atmosphere, Molly pranced and moved away, causing Amber to land more heavily in the saddle than she'd intended.

"Sorry girl," she said, giving a tug on the reins to ask Molly to stand still, "but you were supposed to stand still, remember?"

Molly snatched at the reins but Amber resisted the pony's determination to take over and start moving. "No girl. We're just going to stand here and relax like we practised." Amber slumped in the saddle and loosened her reins again to encourage Molly to soften and unwind, as they'd been rehearsing at home.

Molly was in no mood for the lesson that day, and pawed the ground, impatient to get moving towards the sounds of adventure in the distance. Amber didn't pat her, but she spoke to her soothingly and tried to keep her own body loose and relaxed. Eventually, although she was still trembling with eagerness to get going, Molly finally stood still on a loose rein.

"Good girl. Now we can go." Amber patted Molly gently as she allowed the restless pony to move on.

As she rode onto the track that led to the collecting ring, congratulating herself for her composure, Amber became aware of another rider drawing up beside her. She stole a quick look to her left and quickly wished she hadn't. It was Elisha-girl. Seeing her immediately irked Amber.

The girl's pony wasn't what Amber expected. Because she had turned into Elisha Templeton in Amber's mind, she'd expected her to be on a sleek equine athlete, like Elisha's North Quest or Thunder Cat, but this girl's pony was a feathery skewbald. He wasn't heavily built, but he was at least part-cob and his rider had to push him on to keep up with Molly's long, graceful stride.

"Heard it's not being going too well for your team so far today," the girl said.

Amber ignored her and didn't reply.

"A shame about one of you being eliminated, like. It puts the pressure on the two of you still to go, doesn't it?" Getting no answer from Amber, the girl continued. "Our first two riders have both gone clear."

"Bully for them," Amber said, more too herself than the girl, trying to keep her cool.

"Did your friend find her bridle?" the girl asked. "Weird that it went missing right before her round."

"How'd you know about that?" Amber bristled, whipping round to look at the girl, who arranged her face into a picture of innocence.

"Oh, you know. I heard you'd all been looking for it."

Amber turned back around and rode on in silence. It was possible that she was telling the truth.

"Of course," the girl's voice floated up behind her. "She really should take better care of her stuff and not leave her tack locker open at big events like this."

She kicked her pony on and trotted past Amber, calling over her shoulder. "You never know who's around, do you?"

– Twenty –

The Last Laugh

"And this is the third rider from the Blakefield junior girls' team: Amber Anderson on Just Molly."

Amber pushed Molly straight out of the start box, as if she was riding into battle. In a way, she was. Elisha-girl had succeeded in messing up Chelsea's round, and the fact that she'd all but confessed she'd taken Skye's bridle was clearly meant to unsettle and demoralise Amber before hers.

You may think you've won, Amber told the girl, in her head, *but you're not having the last laugh. You're not manipulating me.*

Amber was fighting back. That girl was not going to get a better riding score than she was. She had run faster and swum further than Amber, but the riding phase was where the most points could be earned. And Amber was aiming to get the full 1,400 points on offer. She wasn't going to seize up with nerves, or doubt herself or her pony. The new Amber was on board now and was ready to kick on.

Molly relished the change in her rider's attitude. Today they were a team, with one shared goal. Molly sensed no fear or apprehension from her rider, just adrenaline and fierce resolve. They shot out of the start box with purpose and were over the telegraph poles and the hanging log into the woods, out of sight of the spectators, in seconds.

Amber steadied Molly as they landed into the wood as the track sloped downhill to a natural stream at the bottom, which was flagged as the third obstacle. Molly barely got her hooves wet as her long stride carried her over it. Amber enjoyed the brief cool provided by the leafy trees as they followed the track before they emerged into another field for the next two obstacles. Fence four was one that Amber knew poor Honey would have struggled with. It was a bank to be jumped up onto, followed immediately by a rail. There was no room for the pony to take a stride: it was a bounce fence and required power.

Amber gave Molly a steadying aid to make sure she had seen and assessed the obstacle ahead of her, but kept her leg on to maintain the impulsion. Molly understood perfectly and powered up onto the bank and over the rail as if they were nothing. Next, they were taking the jump the girls referred to as the 'Cottesmore Leap,' as the huge brush fence with an open ditch in front of it reminded them of the legendary Burghley fence. Amber gasped as Molly soared over it and accelerated up the hill into the next field.

Amber pushed on to avoid getting any time faults, and she hoped it might tire the pony briefly, making her more cooperative at the gate. She needn't have worried. At the top of the hill, Molly flew over the red-roofed house fence but then allowed herself to be slowed back to a trot as they headed over to the gate in the hedgerow that separated the field from the one next door.

The gate was hung from the left, meaning that it was easier for a rider to open it with their left hand. JoJo, Chelsea and Emily hadn't been pleased to see this, but Amber couldn't have been happier. Not only was she now practically ambidextrous due to the increased use of her left hand, since breaking her right collar bone, the gate into the small paddock at the farm was also left-handed.

Amber guided the pony into the position they'd practised at the farm. Molly now understood what was being asked of her when she was presented at a closed gate. Amber deftly lifted the rope with her left hand and pushed Molly forward at the same time that she leaned over and opened the gate. Using the aids for a turn on the forehand, she was able to quickly manoeuvre Molly around the gate without ever having to let go of the rope. Dropping it back securely over the gate stoop, she turned the pony back in the direction of the course and continued.

The next fence was the double of angled rails at the bottom of the hill. Not wanting to make Chelsea's mistake, she made sure she had control of Molly as they reached the first part and, as they soared over it, she opened her left rein and kept her right leg on to signal where they were going next. The pony locked on to the next fence and jumped it at an angle, wasting no time getting back up to speed.

Fence nine was cut into the hedgerow that separated this field from the next. It was enormous, and the ground on the landing side was lower than on the take-off side. As they began to tilt towards the ground, Amber's mouth became a perfect 'O' as they nose-dived from a tremendous height.

The next fence was one of the scariest on the course: the main fence was a drop down off a ledge into the next field, but it was a huge drop. When Amber had first seen it on the course walk, she couldn't believe her eyes or imagine herself riding that fence. The girls had nicknamed it the 'Leaf Pit' after another famous Burghley fence. There was an alternative: a drop down from a lower ledge followed by an arrowhead. Amber would have loved to take the lower drop, but she had vowed not to take any alternatives. She was going for full marks.

So, pulling Molly back to a trot again, she approached the steeper of the drops. Screwing her eyes up so that she couldn't look down, she lengthened her reins and kept nudging Molly forward. Molly baulked at the sight of the huge drop ahead of her, but not wanting a hesitation to cost her sixty penalties, Amber urged her on with seat, legs and voice. "Go on!" she begged.

Molly obliged and slithered her way off the ledge. It was a somewhat bumpy landing, but Amber patted her and pushed on. They needed to get their impulsion back up for the next fence: a picnic table.

Molly was soon back into her stride and flew the picnic table with ease before negotiating the skinny roll tops and galloping up another hill to a tiger trap set into the hedgerow which took them into yet another field. The first fence they met here was the terrifying trakehner which Amber had vowed not even to attempt when she saw it on the course walk. But both Chelsea and Emily had taken it on and cleared it at the first attempt so she knew she had to try too.

"Go on girl!" Amber didn't want to let her fears be known to Molly so she rode as if she meant it. She rode so positively that she knew if Molly refused this fence, she was going to end up in the ditch. But she was too far committed to back out at the last minute. She felt Molly's shoulders lift and they were up and flying! Amber couldn't believe they were over it. Elation raced through her blood, but there was no time to get carried away. The most dreaded obstacle on the course was next: fence fifteen was the slip rail.

"Woah girl." Amber coaxed Molly to slow down and kicked her feet out of the stirrups as they approached the rail, to signal that they were not to jump it. Amber's heart performed a tribal dance as if to remind her that she was facing her worst fear. She fumbled with the top rail and led Molly through it. Replacing the rail with shaking hands, Amber kept Molly facing it, as Caroline had told her, rather than turning her to face the direction they were about to go. She knew she only had one minute to remount, but she hesitated. Amber told herself she was pausing so as not to fluster or upset her pony, but she knew that wasn't the real reason.

"Good lass, stand now," she instructed. But although she knew what she had to do; her nerve failed her. She couldn't do it. Molly's blood was up and she was already itching to turn around and carry on.

"No girl, stand still." Amber used the reins to guide Molly back into the position she wanted her. But Molly did not want to stand still and she made to turn around again.

Amber's heart was now hammering so hard, she worried it might crack a rib. *Oh no! What should I do?* In her mind, she saw herself lying broken on the cold hard ground as Molly sped away from her. She couldn't put herself through that again.

Amber was paralysed by uncertainty as time ticked away. *Do I ask the fence judge to hold her for me?* She so wanted to ask for help but the thoughts of sixty penalties, Honey's eye and the deal she'd made to make it get better, and the Elisha-girl's scorn stilled her.

You can do this, Amber. She heard Caroline's voice and pictured her standing beside them, smiling her encouragement. This was it. Her chance to make Caroline, and her dad, and everyone proud of her. She was not going to blow it.

"STOP IT!" she yelled at Molly, yanking her back to where she wanted her to stand. "Now stand *STILL*." Molly flinched and rolled her eyes but did as she was told. Amber got her foot in the stirrup and was almost in the saddle when Molly decided that she just couldn't wait any longer.

Fortunately for Amber, Molly swung to the left, rather than the right, which brought her underneath Amber's raised right leg. She was back in the saddle, albeit without her right stirrup, when Molly launched herself into a gallop.

"No!" Amber screamed in terror, gripping onto the saddle with her knees, desperately trying to gather up her reins to stop Molly's flight. The next fence, the beer barrels, were approaching, and Amber still didn't have her right stirrup. She couldn't pull up now though as she was on course for the fence. She would be deemed to have 'presented' at it and, if she pulled up or turned a circle now, it would earn her sixty penalties. She just had to go for it and hang on.

Molly was going far too fast, partly out of excitement and partly because her rider's fear was contagious. She messed up her stride at the barrels and nearly tipped herself over. She caught a toe on the way up and it made her twist her body as she arced over the fence.

"Aaaaarrrgghhh!" screamed Amber, as she lost her balance and slipped to the right. As soon as Molly landed from the barrels, Amber pulled on the right rein with all her might to stop the pony bowling on and leaving her on the ground. "STOP!" she roared.

The Blakefield supporters on the bank couldn't see Amber but they were gripping each other tightly as they listened to the commentator's report.

"And it seems as if Blakefield rider, Amber Anderson, is having some trouble on the course," he announced, sounding pleased to have something out of the ordinary to comment on. "It looks like Just Molly didn't want to wait for her rider at the slip rail and has set off for the barrel fence before she was mounted. Amber is now on board, but looking a bit out of control as they head to the barrels, and, oops! Just Molly nearly took a tumble there! Good golly, a bit too keen there, I think Miss Molly!"

Mr and Mrs Anderson clutched each other at the "oops!"

"I knew we couldn't trust that pony!" Mrs Anderson cried. "Please don't let her hurt our Amber again."

"And they're alright. I'm hearing that Just Molly has received some stern words from her rider and they've just gone straight through the troublesome double of corners. No alternative needed by this pair. And now, for the Colfer Farmers Hunt, South branch, we have Keira Marshall-Digby just starting on Double Dare"

The commentator broke away from Amber, leaving her supporters on tenterhooks, but they didn't have to wait for long as they soon saw her come splashing through the water jump back into the home field. Molly opened up and raced for the final fence, fresh as a daisy. She cleared the flower box with feet to spare and had to be pulled up after she'd galloped through the finish. She wasn't tired at all.

"How was it? Were you clear?" Friends, family and teammates surrounded her, looking up at her with concern.

"It... was... interesting," Amber puffed. "But yeah, I think we were clear!"

"Yes!"

"Brilliant!"

"Whoo-hoo, cock-a-doodle-do!"

A wave of congratulations crashed over her, as she slipped from Molly's side and looked at her pony. "You bad girl," she said, ruffling Molly's forelock. "But you did good." Molly's nostrils were flared, showing the pink membranes within, and her eyes were wide and bright. She looked so alive, so vital and full of spirit, as if she was ready to go and do it all again. It was a look that both terrified Amber and warmed her heart. Molly never looked like that when they went show jumping. At shows she looked dull and bored.

"What am I going to do with you?" Amber asked her. Molly nudged her in answer.

"What's that supposed to mean?" Amber said, pulling a Polo mint out of her breeches pocket, which the pony crunched up happily.

"I'll give her a walk around to cool her off," Mr Anderson said, taking the reins from Amber. "Here's a drink and then you can get out of all that hot, sweaty gear. That's you done. We'll put Molly away and then there's just Jo to go."

Amber gratefully handed the reins over to her father and downed the contents of the bottle in one gulp. She would go and sit with everyone else to listen to JoJo's round, but it wasn't her priority. It was practically a fact that JoJo would get a clear round.

Right then, at that moment, Amber wanted to take in what she'd achieved. After all the problems and months of worry about Molly and which pony she should ride, as well as the fretting about her performance matching the others in the team, it was all behind her. She'd trained hard and it had paid off. She knew she wasn't as good as Chelsea or JoJo, but that didn't matter: she'd held her own. She felt that she'd deserved her place on the team and contributed well to it. She'd overcome every challenge that had been thrown at her. It had been exhausting, but now all the stress and anxiety were behind her, she could see what she'd accomplished.

Thinking back to how she believed she didn't belong in the Pony Club on Pearl, how Honey was looked down on by Elisha Templeton as being 'the wrong type of pony for competing', how Molly had left her dreams of red ribbons and trophies in tatters, she couldn't believe how far she'd come.

Amber laughed. It didn't matter what anyone thought about her or her ponies. It didn't matter about red ribbons or trophies. She had three ponies that she loved, each in their own way. Whatever the result of this competition, Amber was happy.

- Twenty-One -

An Unexpected Gift

Amber was right about JoJo's cross-country round: it ran like clockwork. The commentator's report was a repetition of, "Joanne Jones for Blakefield branch, clear at fence four, the bank and rail." All that changed was the fence number. In no time at all, JoJo was back, cantering serenely through the finish as if she'd just been for a gentle hack.

"I don't know how she does it," Amber said incredulously to Emily and Chelsea, as they sat on the bank and clapped JoJo through the finish. "She makes it look so easy. My round was slightly more hair-raising."

"Yeah, but at least it was interesting to listen to." Emily punched her lightly on the arm. "We were all 'oohing' and 'ahhing' and grabbing onto each other, listening to your round." She demonstrated by suddenly seizing Amber, making her gasp. "You nearly gave us all heart failure. And at least you didn't miss a stinking great fence out like me, and get yourself eliminated."

"I know. You're such a loser Teepee," Amber joked. Emily's eyebrows disappeared into her fringe and she laughed, poking Amber in the ribs.

"Get you, giving it some bants!" she chuckled.

Amber hugged her, pulling Chelsea in too. "Love yous."

"Gerroff!" Chelsea resisted the hug, although she was secretly loving it, delivering a playful punch of her own.

"Ow!" Amber rubbed her arm. "Never mind CC as your nickname. Chelsea – The Crusher – Connor would be better for you. You should go into boxing or wrestling next. You'd be a natural."

When the results were revealed later in the day, everyone was sunburned, thirsty and tired. But happy. The results were almost incidental.

Amber was stunned to find that she'd come fourth individually, thanks to the full marks in the riding phase.

192

She'd worried that she might have been given a stop at the bank when Molly hesitated, or that she could've taken too long to remount at the slip rail. But no; she'd been given a clear round and awarded the full 1,400 marks, as well as a special black rosette trimmed in gold for doing so.

JoJo, of course, was the overall winner of the individual junior girls. She also got a black rosette, as well as a huge silver trophy, plus two additional medals for getting the highest score in the shoot and the swim too.

"A very impressive score, young lady," said the tweedy man who presented the prizes. "You should see if there are any Pony Clubs in your area running triathlons. You're good enough to be selected for regional competitions, you know. You could make it onto the North of England Tetrathlon team." He gave her a wink as he handed her the trophy, engraved with the names of decades' worth of past winners.

In the team event, they just missed out on the win, which went to Elisha-girl's team. Their three members whose scores were counted had come second, third and fifth individually. Amber was delighted that Elisha-girl, who was actually named Keira, had come fifth, meaning that she was behind Amber, but Chelsea looked murderous that Keira was ahead of her. Amber and Emily surreptitiously steered her away before she did Keira some harm. It didn't help that the winning team immediately started talking and giggling loudly about the Tetrathlon Championships they would now go on to in August to take on all the other winners from areas around the country.

"You'll be going to that as an individual," Chelsea said to JoJo, allowing herself to be steered away from the winning team's celebrations. "So, make sure you win that as well."

"Oh, ha ha! Can you imagine being the winner of the championship?" JoJo laughed, with uncharacteristic modesty. "It'd be like winning an Olympic medal!"

The next day was a Monday but Amber was able to enjoy a well-earned lie-in as it was the first day of the summer holidays. By the time they eventually bumped up the farm track to see the ponies, it was nearly lunchtime.

Amber gave Molly a hug and a face full of kisses before turning her out into the paddock for a leg stretch. Her mother had still been chuntering about Molly not being safe all the previous evening, following her performance at the slip rail, but Amber had defended her pony.

"We've only just started trying to reschool her out of that, Mum. She's been doing well, but she needs more practice. Caroline says it can take months to properly reform a habit, especially a well ingrained one."

"Oh, *Caroline says*, does she?" Mrs Anderson joked. She heard a lot of 'Caroline says' as Amber hung on to her every word and quoted her advice several times a day without fail.

"Yes, she *does*," Amber replied, not appreciating her mother's teasing. "Because it's true."

Once Molly was happily pulling at the grass in the small paddock, Amber helped her mother to muck out and apply the drops to Honey's eye. It was looking less weepy and cloudy, but it wasn't fully healed yet. "It will heal though," Amber whispered to Honey, laying her face against the pony's and smoothing her long forelock. "I made a deal with the horse gods: Neptune, Epona, Rhiannon... if I conquered my fear, and survived riding Maniac Molly in the Tetrathlon, they would heal your eye and give you your sight back." She kissed Honey on the nose. "And I did, so you'll be better soon."

Leaving Mrs Anderson to take Kasper for a little walk, Amber saddled Pearl and headed out for a ride with JoJo.

As they rode along the track towards the forestry, breathing in the summery scent of cut grass as tractors rumbled in the fields around them, all busy baling hay, it was like old times. She was on Pearl and JoJo was back on Flash. He was being brought back into work and was allowed to go out on short, slow hacks to test his soundness. Flash seemed to have other ideas about the slow part, and was jogging and tossing his head, as usual.

"Jeez. After all he's been through, he's just the same!" JoJo chuckled as the pony snatched at his reins and tried to break from his jog-walk into a trot.

"He's probably just pleased to be back out and about again, on such a lovely day too," Amber suggested. "What's... er... the plan for him now?" she asked.

"Well, Matthew needs something with a bit more 'go', now that he's ready to move on from Sam, but I'm not sure if Flash might have a bit too much 'go' and not enough 'woah' for him. That's what we need to find out."

"I bet you're chuffed to have won the Tetrathlon?" Amber said, changing the subject.

"Yeah, it was brilliant. I still can't believe it."

"Are you... feeling a bit better about things now? You've been pretty quiet recently. You're like JoJo without the mojo!"

JoJo held her head up, that small action making her seem more like the girl Amber knew.

"Yeah, well I don't have to see anyone from school for six weeks now, at least, so hopefully by the time we go back, people will have forgotten about it and there'll be some new gossip for them all to latch on to."

JoJo was putting on a brave face, but Amber could see that she'd been hurt by it. Her friend was usually bold, bossy and self-assured, but lately she'd seemed to fade away. It was astonishing really that she'd managed to perform so well physically when she'd been suffering so much emotionally. Amber told her as much.

"Well, I had you to inspire me, didn't I?" JoJo replied, not looking in Amber's direction.

"You *what*? *You're* inspired by *me*? How? There's nothing inspiring about me! More like the other way around!"

"Of course there is, idiot." JoJo kept her eyes on the track ahead of her. "I see you looking at Emily and

197

Chelsea, trying to be like them, and probably me as well. But you don't need to do that." She sneaked a quick look over at Amber to gauge her reaction. Amber looked as shocked as she'd expected she would.

"Oh yeah! The hair, the teeth, the sporting prowess and social magnetism: I'm great. I can really see why you'd look to me for inspiration," Amber replied, disbelief giving her words an edge of sarcasm.

"Don't do that."

"What?"

"Put yourself down like that. You won't have braces forever and you could get straighteners for your hair if you want. But those things don't matter anyway."

"Ha! Says you, who looks like you do!" Amber retorted.

Finally, JoJo looked at her. "God, you're annoying!"

Amber turned her face away, ready to sulk for the rest of the ride. She heard JoJo let out a frustrated sigh beside her, then she spoke quietly. "It's your bravery and your determination that have been inspiring, if you want to know."

Amber's head snapped around without her even thinking about it. "Brave? Me? What are you talking about? I'm not brave. I'm terrified of everything most of the time. You and Emily are brave, riding ponies like Flash and Pink without batting an eyelid. Chelsea's brave, standing up for me while I just stood there like a dummy. How on earth am I brave?"

"Because…" JoJo explained patiently, "you've stuck with Molly and kept on and on trying with her, even though you've been scared of her at times. You could have just sold her and got something else. Loads of people would have. But you didn't. Even when she landed you in Brantfort's swamp, you got back on and finished and did the show jumping too. That was so amazing! It's like you're loyal to her, and you're determined and, even though you were scared of letting the team down, or embarrassing yourself, or whatever, you still kept going… so I figured, if you could stay positive and not give in, then I wouldn't either. But, you know, in a different way. I'm not going to let those horrible girls I thought were my friends win. I'm going to be a Tetrathlon champion. You know there's an international Tetrathlon exchange for riders once you get to sixteen? That's what I'm aiming for."

Amber stared at JoJo for a moment, lost for words. "OMG, are you, like, psychic or something? How did you know that was how I was feeling?"

"You don't exactly have a poker face. You're pretty easy to read."

"Oh!" Amber exclaimed.

"But that's a good thing. That's what I like about you. It means you're honest. You're straightforward; you don't play games. You're just you. And you should be happy to be you. You don't need to compare yourself to other people and try to be like them. It's them that should try to be more like you!"

Amber couldn't reply. Her eyes had suddenly brimmed with unexpected tears and her throat was burning. JoJo, her friend with the perfect French plaits, tumble turns, and all-round champion, was going to far eclipse her and leave her behind, but Amber didn't mind. She'd just given her the best gift anyone could. It was worth far more than any trophy or prize in a competition: JoJo had seen something in her that was admirable, that had inspired her.

To Amber, that was the best thing anyone could've given her. She knew that she'd remember this moment for the rest of her life.

Author's Note

Believe it or not, it's true that the scariest thing for me about Tetrathlons was doing the slip rail! That time when Molly ran away with me while I was trying to get on, leaving me with a broken collar bone, stayed with me long after. Even years later, when I'd graduated onto horses, I worried about slip rails more than anything.

In reality, the year I did an Area Tetrathlon with Molly, it was held somewhere in Scotland. Back then, my

Pony Club – Wyndham – was part of Area 19, rather than Area 2, as it is now. I can remember walking the course with my parents and my mother being unable to believe the height of the fences I had to take on. She couldn't watch my round! But despite all the problems I had with Molly, we did get round.

She was a pony who showed me what it means to face your fears. I know now, having ridden so many different horses (Molly was my last pony – after her, I went on to horses. You can find out about that in book 5!), that Molly and I weren't best suited. We didn't click in the way that makes some horses feel like a second skin – a part of you – but I'm pleased to have found out that she did experience that relationship with other owners she had in her lifetime.

All those feelings that Amber has in this book – the self-doubt, the need to fit in, to measure up, to be good enough, were all the things I remember feeling at the time. But it was the beginning of me learning to accept myself. There are always going to be people who are better at things than you (unless you're lucky enough to be a JoJo!), so comparing yourself to others isn't helpful. Sometimes you have to keep your eyes on your own lane and concentrate on doing the best you can. Accept your weaknesses, whilst doing what you can to improve them, of course. But also, accept your strengths. We've all got some. If you're like Amber, you might find it difficult to know what you're good at and what other people admire about you. They don't often tell you! But trust me – there's something. So, just be you. You never know who's watching you and wishing they could be like you because you inspire them.

Acknowledgements

This book has probably had more input and support from a range of people than any of the others in the Amber's Pony Tales series. I'm so grateful to everyone for the part they played.

The last time I competed in a Tetrathlon was in 1998. I still have very clear memories of the sport as I took part in team events at branch and Area level for several years, but I was worried that it might have changed over the last 20 years and that my recall of it might now be out of date. I needed to consult with people who know the sport in the present time to make sure I wrote about it accurately. I'd like to thank Kaylee Clark, Carol Elliot and Emma-Kate Darnton for answering my questions and providing me with up-to-date information.

In addition, several Tetrathletes acted as beta readers and advisers on the manuscript: Olivia Graham from Newcastle and North Durham Pony Club and Zara Bowden, from the South Durham Pony Club, who are both highly experienced Tetrathletes, as well as Chloe

Johnson, Lucy Melcher and Emily Dick. Thank you, girls, for all your positive and constructive feedback. Thanks also go to Pony Club Tetrathlon Chairman, Tim Vestey who enthusiastically agreed to read the pre-publication manuscript too. It was such an invaluable resource to have people who are currently involved with the sport to make sure the story reflected their experiences accurately.

I'm grateful to Mark Clague for his advice on the symptoms and treatment of uveitis and eye ulcers in horses after his horse, Jordy, had the misfortune of experiencing it.

Once again, thanks to Katie Trotter for allowing her pony, Clyde, to reprise his role as cover star – and for taking the picture you see on the cover of this book. And, of course, the same goes for Strawberry, courtesy of Myla Postlethwaite-Todd.

Final thanks go to Amanda Horan at Let's Get Booked for editing, formatting and cover design, and Mel Avery, June Haraldsen and Martyn Robinson for their fantastic services as proof readers, spotting those pesky little errors that had slipped through the net!

For free bonus material linked to this book, plus news, competitions, and exclusive opportunities connected to the author's other books, sign up to the mailing list at www.helenharaldsen.co.uk

Did you enjoy this book? The author would love to see your reviews on Amazon. Please feel free to post your comments and let others know about Amber's Pony Tales.

Follow Amber's Pony Tales on Facebook.

Printed in Great Britain
by Amazon